'Hasn't anyone told you that all the money in the world will not make a joyous marriage?'

With these words Captain Lance Merrick makes it quite clear to Miss Elena Blake that he disapproves of her engagement to the wealthiest bachelor in Savannah. She would do far better to marry *him*, Lance assures her, for he does not want her wealth—only her body, her mind and her heart.

But can Elena, brought up to believe that gold is the most important thing on this earth, hope to find happiness as the pioneering wife of a penniless adventurer?

GW00701572

By the same author in Masquerade

CAMILLA

Savannah Wedding

Sara Orwig

MILLS & BOON LIMITED
London · Sydney · Toronto

First published in Great Britain 1983
by Mills & Boon Limited, 15–16 Brook's Mews,
London W1A 1DR

ISBN 0 263 74485 X

Set in 10 on 11 pt Linotron Times
04/1283

Photoset by Rowland Phototypesetting Ltd
Bury St Edmunds, Suffolk
Made and printed in Great Britain by
Cox & Wyman Ltd, Reading

Historical Note

IN 1802, as a new nation, the United States began westward expansion. Cutting across the length of the land, from north to south, was the Mississippi River which provided means for settlers to get their goods to market. By barge, wheat, flour, hemp, tobacco, hides and furs were floated downstream to Natchez and New Orleans.

Because the Mississippi's currents were too swift for a return trip before the days of steam, boats were broken up and sold for lumber, then rivermen journeyed home by land.

A buffalo trail, later used by the Natchez Indians, cut through the untamed wilderness. This path, or trace, became the trail for people to return north. Rugged, winding through forests and swamps, it was given the nickname, 'The Devil's Backbone'. Along this route explorers, trappers, planters, preachers, soldiers and rivermen gained access to a wilderness and opened vast new lands to settlement.

Traversing five hundred miles from Natchez northward to Tennessee, the Trace was the only means of overland travel for many years and, consequently, a major contribution to America's growth.

In 1806, President Thomas Jefferson ordered the Natchez Trace made into a road 'twelve feet in width and passable for a wagon'. In 1938, by a Congressional act, the Natchez Trace Parkway became a project of the National Park Service. This highway follows the old Trace as a monument to America's history.

CHAPTER
ONE

SAVANNAH
1802

ABOVE moss-draped oak trees, an April moon splashed silvery light over a black carriage. The young coachman urged the two matched chestnut horses to make more speed along the country road approaching Savannah. His two female passengers were in a hurry to get home.

Inside the carriage a woman, greying and plump, peered nervously out of the window, clutching her shawl tightly around her.

'Ma'am, it's disgraceful for you to be out alone at night. Your aunt and uncle would never have allowed it. You really should call on friends earlier in the day.'

On the opposite seat, her young mistress shifted slightly and moved her parasol against the skirt of her silk pelisse. Elena Blake's unusual green eyes rested kindly on Dorset, her maid. 'I hadn't seen Jane for so long, Dorset, I quite forgot the time.'

Any more words on the subject were forgotten as the carriage rounded a bend and a commotion started.

Shouts were heard. A horse neighed with a frantic, shrill whinny while steel clanged against steel. Puzzled, the passengers looked out.

Elena saw two men engaged in a sword-fight. Facing them was a man armed with a musket. Both the man with the musket and one of the swordsmen were masked.

'Saints be!' Dorset gasped. 'Brigands have set upon that man . . .'

Elena decided the man with the musket dared not fire in fear of hitting his companion. As the carriage drew abreast, he turned and aimed the musket at it.

'Now we'll be robbed too!' Dorset cried. The carriage jerked to a halt, sending both women sliding.

Dorset shrieked in terror when the door flew open. A musket was brandished at them and a gruff male voice ordered them out.

'C'mon. Move quickly!'

Elena grasped Dorset's arm, whispering, 'Don't be frightened; we'll be all right.' She gathered the skirts of her pelisse and muslin dress to emerge from the carriage. A silk reticule dangled from her wrist as she turned and reached up to aid Dorset.

While they climbed down, the man with the musket commanded the driver, 'Get down, old man, and un-hitch those horses.'

Elena cried, 'You can't take my horses!'

'You'll be fortunate if we don't take you!' he snapped.

Elena glared at him. She knew to a farthing how much both horses had cost her uncle and she could not bear to part with such expensive horseflesh. In helpless rage she watched the brigand mount and gather the reins to her horses and his companion's horse.

She glanced at the sword-fight. A broad-shouldered man in a black cloak and tricorn wielded his sword with skill. He parried a thrust. With lightning swiftness his sword glinted as he lunged forward. The masked man's sword flew high in the air.

Quickly, the masked man attempted to snatch a pistol from his waistband, but before he could fire it, he was slain by a sword-thrust.

The moment he crumpled to the ground, his companion whipped the horses into a gallop and thundered away. As he went, he raised his musket to aim at the swordsman.

Elena screamed, 'Look out!'

The man in the black cloak dropped to the ground. While he snatched up the fallen pistol, a musket shot blasted the night. To Elena's relief, it missed its mark. As the brigand galloped away, the man in the cloak straightened. He gazed after the fleeing horses before he knelt beside the body on the ground to feel for a heartbeat. Swiftly, he rose and moved forward to meet Elena.

She reached the man in the cloak and gasped, 'The thief is getting away with my horses!'

With a wave of his hand, the man motioned. 'He's gone.' He glanced past her. 'It looks as if I'm needed here.'

She turned to see Dorset stretched on the ground. 'Oh, no! Dorset has fainted. There are salts in the carriage.'

The man slipped off his cloak and dark blue coat to reveal a stain on one white sleeve. Elena noticed it and exclaimed, 'You're hurt!'

He shook his head. 'Nothing serious. Let's see to your companion first.' With long strides he moved to Dorset, picked her up and placed her in the carriage. Stepping down, he faced Elena and removed his hat in a sweeping bow.

'Captain Lance Merrick of the *Seahawk*, at your service.' He replaced his hat atop black curls and gazed at her with curiosity. 'Miss . . . ?'

'Blake,' she finished. She introduced Perkins, her driver and said, 'I'll look at Dorset.'

Instantly Captain Merrick was at her side to help her into the carriage. He entered behind her and seemed to fill the narrow space. Elena searched the small bag Dorset carried and found a bottle of salts.

Captain Merrick raised Dorset's head gently and held

the bottle beneath her nose. He glanced at Elena. 'Do you need a whiff of this?'

'Indeed not! I should like to put a ball through that villain's heart! At least he didn't get away with all our valuables.' She touched the large diamond engagement ring on her finger. It glittered and Captain Merrick asked, 'Are you engaged?'

'Yes,' she replied. 'Let me bind your wound, sir.' She opened her reticule and produced a cambric handkerchief. 'Hold out your arm.'

She was aware of his watchful eyes while she rolled his sleeve. Lean, hard muscles were covered with coppery skin. Blood from a cut on his upper arm had soaked the fine linen. He reached round with his other hand and grasped the shoulder of the garment to tear it slightly.

'Now,' he said, 'you can rip it off completely. It's too uncomfortable to wear.'

Elena did as he instructed. As soon as she had removed the sleeve, she tied the cambric around his wound. 'I don't want to hurt you.'

'You're not.' He watched her hands. 'Who's the fortunate fellow?'

For a moment she was puzzled by his question. When she realised what he wanted to know, she replied, 'Alfred Crowe.'

Captain Merrick's dark brows met as he frowned. 'A trifle old for you, isn't he?'

Elena drew a sharp breath. 'Thank you, Captain, for your aid. We can manage now.'

To her annoyance, he grinned. Before he could speak, Dorset stirred and opened her eyes. She gasped and started to move away from the Captain, but Elena said, 'Dorset, this is Captain Merrick. He routed one brigand and the other was killed.'

Dorset fell back against the seat and placed her hand on her heart. 'Saints be! Thank heavens that evil man with the musket is gone!'

Elena patted Dorset's shoulder. 'We'll be all right, Dorset. Lie back and close your eyes.' She smiled at the maid who had helped raise her since she was a small child.

Captain Merrick's fingers closed lightly around her elbow. He whispered, 'Step outside for a moment.'

Elena followed and glanced at Perkins who was standing at the front of the horseless carriage. He asked, 'Want me to commence walking to town for help, Ma'am?'

'There's no need,' Captain Merrick answered smoothly. He looked down at Elena. 'My horse should be close.' He whistled shrilly. An answering whinny was heard and in a moment a black stallion emerged from the pines.

Captain Merrick gathered the reins, then returned to Elena. She said, 'Perhaps Perkins should go with you.'

'I can't leave two females alone here. You wouldn't have any protection.'

'It might be compromising for my reputation if I ride into Savannah with you.'

'No one will ever know,' he drawled.

She raised an eyebrow while she considered their dilemma. Finally she nodded. 'Very well.' She turned to Perkins. 'I'll send someone for you as soon as possible. Take care of Dorset.'

'Aye, Ma'am,' he replied.

Elena climbed into the carriage. 'Dorset.' She placed her hand on the woman's shoulder. 'I'm going to ride to Savannah with the Captain. I'll send someone to fetch you soon. Perkins will be here.'

Dorset whispered, 'Oh, Ma'am, you don't know this man!'

Elena stated gently, 'Dorset, if I don't go with him, we'll be stranded here until Perkins walks into town. I'll be all right.' She squeezed Dorset's hand and stepped out of the carriage.

After handing Perkins a pistol, Captain Merrick lifted Elena on to his horse. With a lithe movement he swung up behind her, then twisted the reins so his horse would head towards Savannah.

In bright moonlight they moved down the road beneath the spreading branches of many oaks. Elena had never ridden with a man and she was keenly conscious of Captain Merrick's long, lean body behind her.

His voice was low. 'How did old Alfred Crowe ever capture the heart of such a lively young miss?'

'Sir!' she bristled. Even if he had done them a service, the Captain had nerve. ''Tis not one bit of your concern.'

He continued as blithely as if she had willingly answered. 'He is older, far older than your . . .' He leaned back and Elena glanced over her shoulder to discover him regarding her keenly. She turned away while he finished, '. . . your eighteen years.'

'Nineteen,' she stated.

'Nineteen years. He is boorish, dull, taciturn—all the things you are not.'

'He is inordinately rich!' she snapped.

'Oh ho! So that's the attraction.' He spoke in mocking tones. 'Hasn't anybody told you that all the money in the world will not make a joyous marriage?'

She twisted around to face him. 'Sir, it's none of your affair. Will you kindly drop the subject?'

'Ah, but I find it absolutely fascinating.' He observed her. 'Golden hair, mischievous green eyes, rosy cheeks and the softest skin . . .'

She wriggled uncomfortably and felt her cheeks flame. 'You have gone beyond the bounds of decorum!'

His arm slipped around her waist. 'I intend to go further.'

He lowered his head quickly and his lips brushed hers. Elena pushed against his chest. His arm tightened and he raised his head a fraction to look at her. 'I'd say Alfred hasn't taught you much about kissing.'

Elena shook with fury and fear. Fear began to dominate as he leaned closer.

'Captain! How dare . . .'

His mouth silenced her protests. With languorous insistence he awakened her to a wry knowledge that he was correct in his analysis of Alfred Crowe's kisses.

Never had she been kissed in such a manner. For an instant she forgot her anger, forgot the dilemma—everything.

She could not breathe; her heart hammered loudly. He released her reluctantly, while beneath the tricorn a lock of black hair tumbled on his forehead.

Awareness of his bold actions and of her own responses, flooded her with embarrassment and fury. She started to slap him and the quick movement unseated her.

A yelp of surprise escaped her lips as Elena reached out to grasp the horse's mane. A strong arm closed around her waist and caught her.

He pulled her up on to the horse again and laughed. 'Careful, Miss Blake.'

'How dare you!'

He stated drily, 'Alfred won't get worked up about it. The only thing that would get Alfred Crowe in an uproar is for the price of his tobacco to fall.'

She squinted at him angrily and with fright. Suppose this man were a friend of Alfred's and informed him about the kiss! She asked, 'How do you know him?'

'I buy his tobacco to sell in England.'

Elena bit her lip. Anger was dissolved into worry. If Captain Merrick mentioned the kiss . . .

Her thoughts were interrupted. He said, 'Never fear, Miss Blake. I wouldn't dream of telling Alfred about the kiss.'

She straightened and stared at the road while she wished the moon would go behind a cloud. It was sufficiently clear for him to see the colour in her cheeks. She stated haughtily, 'Do not make it sound as if I had one thing to do with it!'

His chuckle aggravated her further. He mused, 'Blake . . . I haven't been in Savannah for eight years now—you would have been a small child, but I don't recall any Blakes.'

Determined to refrain from conversing with the odious man, Elena stared straight ahead.

He laughed. 'And you're not going to help me out either! Very well, Miss Blake, I'll ask Alfred.'

'Don't you dare!' She twisted her head again to look up at him. His face was disturbingly close. He had long, thick lashes which made the deep blue of his eyes even more startling. Even in moonlight she was certain they were the bluest eyes she had ever seen.

He smiled. 'At least, you will have to unbend sufficiently to tell me which house is yours.'

They rounded a crook in the road and Savannah lay ahead. She said, 'Perhaps I should get down and walk home from here.'

'Nonsense! At this late hour we won't see a soul.' He added, 'Also, it's a late hour for a young miss to be travelling over the countryside with only a coachman and a nanny.'

Her lips firmed. 'I've heard all I care to on that subject from Dorset tonight.'

'I hope you learned a lesson,' he said.

'I certainly did. Beware of men!'

He laughed. 'You'll have to tell me which way to your house.'

Resigned, Elena gave directions and prayed she would not meet anyone. As if her fears had conjured it up, a familiar carriage rounded the corner ahead of them. 'Oh, no! There are the Whartons!'

Captain Merrick moved into the shadows beneath a large tree. Quickly he slipped his arm around her waist and lowered her to the ground out of sight of the street.

The sound of horses and carriage faded. As soon as they were gone, Captain Merrick leaned down and lifted Elena. Her hand brushed against his chest and she gasped with pain.

Instantly he apologised and asked, 'What hurts?'

She wiggled her fingers and he took her hand in his. Moonlight shone on white, slender fingers; along her wrist were dark scratches. Embarrassed, Elena said, 'I stepped into a bramble bush when I got off your horse.' She withdrew her hand. 'I can walk home from here.'

'You can, but it wouldn't be half as much fun.' He cocked his head to one side and regarded her. 'What do you do for amusement, Miss Blake? I can't envision Alfred providing any.'

'Do not demean Mr Crowe. I told you he is the wealthiest bachelor in Savannah.'

'That elegant silk pelisse and white muslin don't look as if you need Alfred Crowe's money.'

Ignoring his comment, she pointed ahead. 'There's my home.' The sight of the familiar two-storey house filled her with relief. Never had home looked so appealing. Its shuttered windows were shaded by tall oaks. The yard was dotted with trees; against waxen dark green leaves magnolia blossoms were a vivid white and moonlight lent a soft lustre to walls made of 'tabby', a mixture of burnt shells, sand and water.

When they reached the hitching post, Elena started to jump down, but once more his arm slipped around her waist.

'Miss Blake.'

Her heart pounded as she looked up at him. 'Thank you, Captain Merrick, for coming to our rescue and bringing me home. Now, will you kindly remove your arm?'

'Miss Blake, I'm going to take advantage of you and this situation. Give me a kiss.'

The pounding of her heart became a drumroll in her ears. 'Sir! That's ungentlemanly!'

'I don't give a damn,' he stated flatly.

It was difficult to get her breath. Suddenly he no longer sounded as if he were teasing.

'For all your maidenly protests—I think you enjoyed the last kiss,' he drawled sardonically.

She gasped. 'Of all the . . . Are all Englishmen like you?'

He ignored her question and continued, 'And if you scream or raise too much fuss,' he paused and looked pointedly around, 'all these people will hear and come to see what the commotion is about. Come here.'

He leaned forward and his mouth pressed against hers. Again, Elena was kissed thoroughly and expertly. He shifted a fraction and murmured in her ear, 'Put your arms around me.'

She started to protest, but his mouth covered hers. The kiss lengthened. Elena felt as if she had lost all ability to move. Any thoughts of resistance vanished.

His kiss was delicious and provocative, sending a tingling sensation through her. When he released her, she looked up dazedly.

His grin evoked anger. How could she have acted so foolishly! She pushed against him and dropped to her feet. As she hurried away, her cheeks burned with embarrassment.

'Goodnight, Miss Blake,' he stated softly.

Elena heard his farewell, but she could not bear to glance around for she imagined the mocking laughter in those piercing blue eyes.

Hadley, the butler, opened the door and stepped back. If there was any shock over her appearance, his impassive countenance did not reveal it.

Her face flamed, but she turned to say, 'Hadley, I've had . . . we've had an encounter with brigands.'

'Good heavens!' Above a bulbous nose his brown eyebrows arched with shock.

'I left Dorset and Perkins on the river road. Take the other carriage and horses and fetch them. The ruffians stole my good pair of chestnuts! Please, do hurry. I hate to think of Dorset sitting out there in the darkness waiting to be rescued.'

'Aye, Ma'am.'

Elena headed for her room. She could summon one of the maids to help her change, but she did not want anyone else to see her in her present state. When she reached her room, her feelings were affirmed. One look at the full redness of her lips and the crushed condition of the bodice of her white muslin, indicated just how soundly she had been hugged and kissed. She grew warm all over at the memory.

She thought about the tumultuous past hour and her ride with Captain Merrick. The man was arrogant and reckless and . . . indecent! A shiver ran through her—he was also quite handsome and exciting! She began to pull pins from her hair while she recalled each moment with him.

By the time Hadley returned with Dorset and Perkins, Elena had bathed and changed to a warm gown and robe. As soon as Dorset came upstairs, Elena rushed into the hall to meet her.

'Dorset, are you all right?'

'Aye. I'm glad to be home, Ma'am.'

Elena took Dorset's hand. 'This was my fault and I'm sorry. I should not have remained at Jane's that long.'

'No one came to harm, Ma'am.'

Elena said, 'I asked Betsy to bring you hot tea. She has a bath ready and tomorrow you may remain in bed.'

Dorset smiled and patted Elena's hand. 'Ma'am, you are still the sweet child. Thank you.'

Elena sighed and returned to her room to climb on to a feather mattress. She glanced at the diamond on her finger. Usually it gave her a rush of pleasure to gaze at its glittering brilliance, but tonight it looked cold and a little large for her slender finger. Clearly she recalled the deep baritone voice whispering into her ear, his breath warm against her lobe, '*All the money in the world will not make a joyous marriage . . .*'

She flounced the covers and blew out the candle, then gazed into darkness. She tried to forget Captain Merrick, to think about the Jacksons' dinner party tomorrow evening, but insidiously, her traitorous mind kept shifting back to memories of his passionate kisses. Her heart thudded and she wriggled with guilty pleasure. Embarrassed, she thought of Mr Crowe. He had never tried to kiss her until he had presented her with the diamond. Then it had been a stiff, dull kiss that was easily forgotten.

She recalled how pleased her uncle had been when Mr Crowe had asked for her hand. She thought of her uncle as he used to sit in his favourite wing-chair and discuss affairs of the plantation. Once, he had laid aside his spectacles and gazed at her solemnly. Tufts of grey hair circled his bald head and his pale eyes were red from studying figures. Elena had been helping and when he paused, she glanced up. He said, 'I will have to tell Mr Crowe you have a good mind for tabulating the plantation's costs and gains.' He smiled. 'Mr Crowe, most likely, will not allow a female to have a hand in business matters, but this plantation will be yours, Elena, and you'll never know poverty.' He added, 'You've done well in this match, Elena.'

'I'm glad you're pleased,' she had replied, then they had both returned to their books. Only a short week later Uncle Findley had succumbed to pneumonia.

For an instant Elena felt a twinge of remorse. Right now she was wealthy and totally free. It was exhilarating to do exactly as she pleased without breath of scandal. Everyone knew she would wed Alfred Crowe in two months and settle into a circumspect life under his experienced guidance.

In the future she would have to be more careful about travelling around the countryside after dark. The team of chestnuts was well-matched and a bitter loss. Perhaps, Elena mused, she should learn to use a pistol. Contemplation of Mr Crowe's horror at such a suggestion made her giggle. Finally sleep came.

The next day was spent in preparation for the Jacksons' large dinner party. With eagerness to join her friends, Elena dressed in a low-necked white organdie with a pleated hem and tiny puffed sleeves which revealed creamy shoulders and arms. Dorset combed her hair, parted it in the centre and caught it up behind her head in loops. Elena reached up to touch a strand of lustrous pearls around her neck and noticed the scratches on her wrist.

'Oh, Dorset, my hand looks terrible! Everyone will want to know what happened.'

The maid tied a wide, pink sash around Elena's tiny waist, then straightened. 'You can tell them you were set upon by brigands.'

'Dorset, I shan't at all! I might get a reputation that would be unseemly.'

'Indeed, you might,' Dorset stated sternly.

Elena laughed. 'Oh, Dorset, don't be angry.' She turned to hug the maid.

Dorset's cheeks grew pink, but she smiled and her voice was pleased. 'Be off with ye, Miss Elena, and have a good time. Mr Crowe is downstairs in the parlour.'

She hurried to the front parlour where Alfred Crowe rose to greet her. Elena wondered why the man always looked so solemn, for she could think of few times she had seen him smile, and never once had she heard laughter escape his thin lips. Grey sideburns framed long, sallow cheeks beneath pale brown eyes. His coat sleeve was ravelled, which Elena attributed to his bachelor state, but his clothes were less than fashionable because the man would consider it folly to spend his coppers for frippery.

When she had mentioned the fact to Uncle Findley once, he had shrugged it off. 'Never mind, Elena, I shall settle a sufficient sum on you that you may dress as you please. I have never understood the foolish interest of females in attire.'

While Mr Crowe waited, Elena slipped into a pink and white quilted pelisse, pulled on gloves and picked up a reticule. Together, they headed for his carriage to ride down Bull Street, then around the corner to the party.

It was a short distance to the two-storey frame house. Halting before a portico with Corinthian columns, Mr Crowe helped Elena out of the carriage. A footman announced their arrival and they joined a throng in the Jacksons' large front parlour. Wide doors between front and back parlours had been thrown open giving ample space for many guests. Vivacious, brown-eyed Mary Jackson, Elena's best friend, greeted her.

While the conversation swirled around her, Elena gazed at the elegant mauve Italian silk and Brussels lace curtains which decorated the windows. Their soft hues accentuated the deep brown of Queen Anne furniture.

Three bronze whale-oil lamps with crystal globes were above a mantel which had been painted black three years earlier at the death of George Washington, the country's first president.

Jason sauntered up and greeted Elena and Alfred Crowe. While the circle of chatting guests enlarged to include him, Elena saw Mary's quick glance at her husband and the look that passed between them. Jason's arm slipped around his wife's waist. They had been wed a year and it was obvious that each loved the other deeply.

Jason's greeting to Mr Crowe was cool, but polite, reminding Elena that neither of the Jacksons was pleased with her engagement. After a moment Mary left the group to welcome newcomers while Jason drifted towards another cluster of guests.

Men interested in hearing Alfred Crowe's opinions on spring crops soon surrounded Elena and she slipped away to find some of her friends. With the heat of candles, and the increasing number of guests, it was growing warm. Elena moved to the back parlour where there were fewer guests. Doors to a sun porch were open and she stepped through them. She heard a rustle to her left and turned to look into a familiar pair of deep blue eyes.

CHAPTER
TWO

STARTLED, Elena caught her breath. Captain Lance Merrick greeted her.

How handsome he looked in a black velvet coat with a silver-figured moiré waistcoat and grey doeskin breeches. Her heartbeat quickened and her palms grew damp. They were alone in the sun porch. Suddenly fearful he would think she had hunted him down, she asked, 'Have you seen Mr Crowe?'

He looked amused. 'Yes, and I care not to right now, so do not summon him.'

She raised her fan and murmured, 'My, you're forthright.'

'A quality we seem to share,' he replied.

Her eyes narrowed. 'How would you know that? We're absolute strangers.'

'I seem to recall a request for me to put a ball through the heart of a brigand without any hesitation or maidenly tenderness at all.'

'Oh, do be still!' she snapped and looked around. 'I don't want anyone to know about that.'

'Mmm.' He picked up her hand and gazed at the scratches. 'How have you explained this?'

She jerked her hand away from his. 'I said I hurt it in the carriage door. Will you kindly not make any remarks about our previous encounter?' She was beginning to wish she had never discovered the enclosed porch.

He looked at her brazenly with a directness that was unnerving. 'I've made some inquiries today. You know your behaviour is shocking some of Savannah.'

'What are you talking about?' she asked, but she knew too well.

'You have just lost your guardians—an aunt and uncle. Your aunt died six months ago and your uncle a little over a month now. There will be no guardian appointed because you'll soon wed Mr Crowe. In the meantime, you're galavanting around Savannah in a manner that is shocking society. You are not even wearing mourning.'

'You do go on!' She turned around as if hoping for escape. The sun porch was filled with plants, baskets of ferns, gardenia bushes and camellias which hid its occupants from view of other guests. She started to leave, but his words halted her.

'What were you doing out riding around the countryside after dark last night? You were not keeping a tryst behind Alfred's back were you?'

'How dare you!' she gasped.

He laughed. 'Whoa, Miss Blake! I'm teasing.' His eyes became thoughtful. 'You know, it really isn't safe for you to do that. Do you know how to use a pistol?'

'No,' she replied, unthinkingly voicing what had been on her mind all day. 'I must learn to use one, but Mr Crowe would be horrified to teach me—he would refuse.'

'I wouldn't refuse,' Captain Merrick drawled. 'I'll show you how.'

She looked at him, then drew a quick breath and expelled it in a laugh. 'Perhaps that would be more dangerous than roaming around the country unarmed.'

He grinned wickedly, causing crinkles at the corners of his eyes and suddenly looking younger than he had when sombre. 'I'll teach you how and no one will ever know—it'll be our secret.'

'I said before that we're strangers. How do I know it'll be safe to meet you?'

He shrugged one broad shoulder and stated casually, 'I'm Jason's friend. Mary and Jason both will vouch for me. As a matter of fact, they might even approve of the pistol lessons. Mary can use one quite well.'

He propped his elbow on a tall plant stand and leaned closer to gaze at her. 'Come on, Miss Blake. Let me show you how. Meet me tomorrow morning on the river road to the west. I'll watch for you and stay out of sight until we're away from town.' His blue eyes challenged her. 'Will you?'

She studied him and began to enjoy herself. She gazed at his firm mouth and aquiline nose as she tilted her head and replied, 'That's scandalous!'

'Not if no one discovers what you've done,' he added calmly. 'I imagine everyone is getting accustomed to seeing you traipse around alone.'

For an instant Elena considered his offer. A quiver of excitement coursed through her. She should decline. If it was discovered, it would bring down the wrath of everyone in Savannah except the Jacksons, but those devilish blue eyes dared her. She asked, 'How do I know you'd keep it a secret? You have nothing to lose.'

He held up his hand. 'You have my word on it. I don't care to get engaged in a duel. I'm frank, Miss Blake, but I also mean what I say—I'll keep my word.'

'What time?'

He shrugged. 'Mid-morning . . .' He paused and his gaze went past her. He straightened. 'Ten o'clock. Here comes your intended.'

'Ah, there you are, Miss Blake.' Alfred Crowe entered the porch. 'Evening, Lance.'

Elena looked up as her fiancé joined them and the two men greeted each other. For the first time since she had accepted the proposal of marriage, she felt reluctance. It was as if a pall of gloom had come onto the porch with Alfred Crowe. Elena had been having a good time conversing with Captain Merrick.

Lance said, 'This should be an excellent year for tobacco.'

'Yes, with this President, the plantation owners may benefit,' Alfred Crowe answered.

'The whole nation will prosper. Jefferson is a man of ideas. He's looking west to expansion,' Lance added.

At that moment dinner was announced. Alfred offered his arm and looked down at Elena. 'Come, Miss Blake.'

Captain Merrick fell into step on the other side of Elena and the two men discussed conditions of government while they strolled to the table. With a shock Elena saw that she would be seated between Mr Crowe and Captain Merrick. She looked at Mary questioningly and decided to ask later if that had been done purposely.

Over bowls of crab soup with flaky white meat swimming in cream, butter and sherry, Elena engaged in conversation with Mr Crowe, until someone farther down the table spoke to him and Elena was excluded from the conversation.

Captain Merrick asked, 'How did you come to live with an aunt and uncle, Miss Blake?'

'I was orphaned when three years old; my parents died in a fire. There were no other relatives in England so I was brought to Savannah to live with Aunt Agnes and Uncle Findley. The maid who was with me last night accompanied me from England.' She looked into his blue eyes and asked, 'Where were you born, Captain Merrick?'

'London,' came the bald reply and she wondered if there was anything in his past that he wanted to forget. She was curious about his age; he looked extremely fit and swarthy from life at sea. On his other side sat Lucy Hamilton. Elena was certain Lucy would be quite taken with the dashing Captain. As if to confirm her opinion, Lucy's hand lightly brushed his sleeve and he turned away momentarily.

Over juicy pink ham, golden sweet potatoes, and black-eyed peas with pepper sauce, the Captain turned again to Elena. He leaned closer and whispered, 'You know, Miss Blake, you arrived with Alfred Crowe and you will ride home with him. That gives no breath of scandal, yet you won't be seen alone with me even when I've merely rescued you from brigands. Why is that?'

Elena looked up at him. 'No one would suspect Mr Crowe of any ungentlemanly action. He's like . . .'

Suddenly aware of how much she had revealed, she bit her lip. Her cheeks burned as Captain Merrick grinned impudently.

'He's like . . . what?' he coaxed.

'Never mind!'

He leaned sufficiently close that she could detect faint traces of soap on his clothes. 'You mean he's like a guardian, don't you?' He whispered, 'He's parsimonious, stuffy, and absolutely safe to leave alone with a beautiful young lady.'

She wriggled with indignation and fright that her fiancé would overhear the conversation. She looked at Captain Merrick angrily. 'Keep your voice down! I have changed my mind about tomor . . .'

Lucy Hamilton spoke again to the Captain and he turned away. Elena looked at his back, at the thick, luxurious black hair that was fastened in a *queue* behind his head.

Mr Crowe turned to speak to her and continued conversing with her throughout dinner, then remained at her side until they left.

Elena lost sleep while she tossed and turned and debated whether to join Captain Merrick in the morning or not. She knew full well what she should do, but as the days had passed since her uncle's demise, freedom had become a wondrous thing. Staring into the darkness, she realised how much more she dared to do now than only a few weeks earlier.

The next morning Elena bathed, breakfasted, then dressed in a simple dark blue morning dress. Her fingers shook. She knew she should not meet Captain Merrick, yet all she had to do was recall his merry blue eyes, the deep throaty laughter and strong firm jaw, the air of excitement that seemed to surround him . . .

Rationalising her actions with mental arguments that she did need to learn to use a pistol and that Alfred Crowe would never allow such behaviour, Elena snatched up a bonnet and reticule. She was trembling in fear that Dorset would discover her activity; at the moment she did not want to cope with Dorset's disapproval even though it would be little more than a remark and sour looks.

She hurried to the coach house. Earlier she had asked Perkins to ready the gig and Elena was relieved to see it waiting. She climbed into the open, one-horse carriage and took the reins to turn on to Bull Street.

She passed Johnson Square and reached River Street. Usually she enjoyed driving in this street with its abundance of azaleas, elegant houses and the view of ships' tall masts below the bluff, but today Elena was anxious to escape Savannah. Not until she was out of town did she begin to relax. Her palms were clammy and she felt as if every eye had watched her. She glanced around and expelled her breath. The morning was clear and fresh air was invigorating.

Surprised by hoofbeats, she looked around. From behind a clump of purple myrtle, Captain Merrick rode forward. His mocking grin was infectious and she smiled. In a brass-buttoned, dark green coat and leather breeches with high-top boots, he looked as dashing as he had the night before in elegant dinner clothes.

She halted the gig while he rode up beside her. 'You startled me,' she accused.

He smiled and regarded her. 'You look pretty.'

'Thank you.' She could hear her heart pounding

loudly in her ears. She tilted her head to one side. 'You may be my ruin.'

'I'll make it worth it, Miss Blake.'

She raised her chin and tapped his chest lightly with her driving whip. 'You have an excessive amount of arrogance, Captain Merrick.'

He merely laughed and dismounted. He tethered his horse to the gig, then removed a walnut box and powder horn to place them on the floor of the gig. He climbed inside and took the reins and the whip from her. 'We need to get farther from town.'

He looked down at her. 'I had a long talk with Mary last night after you left.'

'Oh?' He did have the most direct way of looking at her, Elena thought.

'She told me about your aunt and uncle. She said they've raised you to consider wealth the most important thing on this earth.'

'Mary told you that!'

He looked at her quickly. 'Don't get angry with Mary. I wormed it out of her. There had to be some explanation for Alfred Crowe.'

Elena clamped her lips together. She could well imagine him getting the information from Mary. She spoke defensively. 'My aunt and uncle were good to me.'

'That may be, Miss Blake, but there is more to consider in life than wealth.'

'I can't imagine anything quite as important!' she snapped. She gazed into solemn blue eyes. 'Uncle Findley told me always to hang on to my possessions.' She glanced at Captain Merrick again. 'You see, most people don't know, and those who do remember may have good reason not to mention it, but when General Oglethorpe established Savannah, he was given a decree by King Charles. This was to be a buffer between the other colonies and Spain's territories to the south of us.'

'Yes, it still is,' Lance remarked dryly. 'South of here,

Florida is still under a Spanish flag. England and Spain have repeatedly clashed over territorial claims.'

Elena continued, 'General Oglethorpe settled this colony for another reason. It was a charitable effort to give people from debtors' prison another chance.'

'That was 1733! Your uncle would have been a child.'

'He was a young boy—eleven years of age. His father had gone to prison for debts he was unable to meet. Even though Uncle Findley was young he never forgot the hardships. His father was a gambler, a folly which always remained the utmost sin to Uncle. Anyway, at that time in England, if a man could not pay his debts he could be sent to debtors' prison. The whole family could accompany him—and often did, because there was no way for them to pay creditors. Once he was in prison, there was no way for Uncle Findley's father to work off his indebtedness.'

Captain Merrick stated coolly, 'I'm aware of the odious aspects of debtors' prison.'

Elena continued, 'When General Oglethorpe offered this opportunity, the Blakes accepted. The entire family travelled to Savannah. One child died at sea. When they started the colony it didn't work out as Oglethorpe had expected and the first years were hard. Uncle Findley's mother and remaining brother died. He and his father were the sole suvivors in the family. Uncle Findley worked hard all his life until the last few years. He became a wealthy man, but he raised me to value my money.'

Captain Merrick shifted and looked down at her. 'That's all well and good, Miss Blake, to a point, but to wed a dry, penny-pincher like Alfred Crowe is beyond the pale. You're a wealthy young woman in your own right. Your plantation is extremely valuable.'

He reined the horse and jumped down, then lashed the reins to a tree. He returned to lift Elena to the ground.

She was aware of his hands against her waist, of his nearness, the fresh smell of his linen shirt. He untied his horse from the gig and moved him closer to the other horse, then reached into his saddlebag to withdraw a folded piece of leather, hammer and pegs.

There was a clear stretch of land, then a clump of pines. He took the piece of leather and hammer and walked the length of open space to tack the leather to a tree for a target.

He withdrew a box from the carriage and opened it to produce a brace of duelling pistols. Sunlight glinted on silver mountings as he turned a weapon in his hand.

'These have extremely short barrels,' he remarked, 'but they're easier to handle.' He picked up a powder horn to commence loading a pistol. While his strong fingers moved with competent ease over a carved walnut stock, Elena concentrated on his instructions. Finally they faced the target and he handed her a pistol.

She accepted it and he caught her wrist quickly. 'Careful. Always watch where you point it,' he cautioned. He stepped behind her to tell her how to take aim, then said, 'Wait a minute, Miss Blake.' He took the pistol from her hands and looked down at her.

'This gets in my way.' He untied the ribbons to her bonnet. His fingers lightly brushed her chin and throat while she stood closely enough to detect traces of gunpowder on his fingers.

With an accurate toss he sailed the bonnet into the gig, then handed her the pistol again. He moved behind her and closed his fingers over her wrist. Elena could feel the warmth of his body. His breath tickled her ear and it was far more difficult to think about the pistol than about him. She tried to heed his instructions.

The blast was deafening and sent birds scattering. Elena's sorrel mare whinnied frantically. Captain Merrick moved to the horse and caught its bridle while he patted its sleek neck. He said, 'The other pistol is loaded and ready, Miss Blake. Go ahead and fire it while I calm your horse.'

Elena changed pistols and fired once more. Neither shot touched the target. This time the horse made less fuss while the Captain softly talked to it.

He left the horse and returned to watch Elena load the pistols. Whenever she started to do something wrong, his fingers would close over hers and he would patiently show her the correct way.

She practised firing half a dozen shots before she finally struck the target, then she hit it twice more out of the next four shots.

He smiled and took the pistol from her hands. 'You are an apt pupil. We'll stop for a while.' He crossed to his horse and removed a blanket from behind the saddle. Elena stood rooted to the ground while she watched him. If anyone caught her sitting on a blanket with Captain Merrick, her reputation would be destroyed forever. What she had already done was bad enough; she knew she should climb into the gig and return to Savannah immediately. 'I'd better go.'

He looked at her and laughed. 'Miss Blake, this morning when you rode out of Savannah alone, you threw over the traces!' He reached out and took her arm. 'Come on,' he coaxed.

She faced him quietly, but a tumultuous debate raged in her thoughts. Elena had been brought up in a strict manner; she knew what she should do. She also knew what she wanted to do. All too soon she would be wed to Alfred Crowe and moments like this would be forever lost. She smiled and sank down on the blanket.

He crossed to his horse again and removed a bottle and flagons from his saddlebag, then sat down. 'I brought cold cider.'

He pulled off his green coat and flung it down. His linen shirt was laced across his broad chest. Never before had she been alone with a man in such a manner and

Elena's pulse quickened. She asked, 'How did you get to be a sea captain?'

'I was impressed—clubbed on the head at night on a London street and hauled away to a ship. The next thing I knew, I was on the high seas in the service of His Majesty. The Royal Navy is filled with men "signed on" in such circumstances.'

'How dreadful!' She sipped the refreshing cider and gazed at him.

He shrugged. 'I was slightly foxed at the time. The press gang probably thought I was fair game.'

She asked, 'If you were impressed into the Royal Navy, why are you in Savannah? There are no Loyalist ships here now, nor any of the Royal Navy.'

He replied, 'I jumped ship and went on board a pirate ship. Before long I had enough capital to outfit my own. Now I own four vessels.'

She looked at him in surprise. 'You own four?'

'Why, Miss Blake, I do believe I see visions of wealth in your big green eyes!'

Embarrassed and angered, she snapped, 'Four ships are a large investment.'

His voice was filled with amusement. 'You sound as if you have an idea of exactly how large it is.'

She wriggled uncomfortably. 'Well, Uncle Findley considered purchasing a ship at one time. He would discuss those things with me. Aunt Agnes had no head for figures.'

'And you do?'

She glanced up at him from beneath lowered lashes. 'Uncle Findley said that I do.'

'That's one thing you and Alfred will have in common, although if he shares any information with you about his finances, it will be most amazing. I doubt if Alfred could ever credit the female mind with ability to cope with anything more complicated than baking cakes,' he stated dryly.

'You don't like Mr Crowe, do you?'

'*Au contraire!* Alfred Crowe is a tight-fisted, solemn man. I don't mind doing business with him—but he's incredibly dull as a companion for a lively young woman.'

'That is my business, Sir. I know what I want.'

He smiled innocuously. 'Do you think Paris is an exciting city?'

Relieved that he was willing to change the subject, she replied, 'I wouldn't know. I've never been there.'

He gazed at her intently. 'That's what you're doing in this engagement. You don't know what other men—or actually any men—are like.'

She started to rise. 'Sir . . .'

He grasped her wrist and smiled. 'Sit down. I'll be quiet on that subject.' He released her and gazed around. 'It's too beautiful a day to return to town. I love the country.'

'Did you grow up in London, Captain Merrick?'

His blue eyes shifted and met hers briefly. 'Part of the time. Do you have any memories of London?'

She shook her head. 'No. I can remember so little.' She regarded him with curiosity. 'You said you jumped ship . . .'

His teeth flashed in a broad grin. 'Aye—and I broke the law,' he admitted. 'I'm subject to arrest and to hang if the British catch me.' His smile faded and he glanced around. 'Savannah was under British rule longer than most. It wasn't many years ago that this was a battle-ground between Colonials and Loyalists. There is still Loyalist sympathy here and this Governor cares little for my presence.'

She was thoughtful. 'That means you can never return to England.'

'That's correct—not unless I want to hang.'

She studied him. 'Do you have family there?'

For the first time in their acquaintance, there was one

brief flash of pain or perhaps anger in his eyes. Elena could not decide which, but she realised she had struck a raw nerve. Whatever it had been, impassiveness replaced it quickly, but he did not answer with his usual lightness and she wondered what had disturbed him.

He said abruptly, 'No family in England.' She could not mistake the bitterness in his voice. Silence stretched between them, then she spoke softly.

'You've asked me all sorts of personal questions, yet . . .' Her voice trailed away.

He looked at her intently and prompted, 'Yet . . . ?'

'You won't answer mine,' she stated in a rush. Her heart thudded at the audacity of her statement. Never had she discussed with any man other than Uncle Findley anything but the lightest subjects.

Captain Merrick gazed at her solemnly. 'I did answer, Miss Blake.'

The words came out before she thought. 'But not truthfully.' She looked into his deep blue eyes and knew she was correct, but she wondered why she felt that way.

He replied quietly, 'My family disinherited me. My father is a wealthy man. He gambled, he drank and he worried my mother to death. He met a young woman who had been married at seventeen, then widowed at twenty-one. She was wealthy, spoiled and beautiful.'

Elena gazed at him while he talked. He spoke in a flat, unemotional voice, yet she had a suspicion he was revealing something to her that he rarely talked about. She listened attentively while he continued.

'They were wed, had a wedding trip and he brought her home. I was the oldest child and only son—at the time I was nineteen years old.' He gazed at her steadfastly and his eyes became glacial. Suddenly she wished she had not asked.

He said, 'My father's new wife found me attractive and she made it abundantly clear. When I rejected her, she went to my father with a tale that almost caused my demise.' He let out his breath and his tone changed. 'Anyway, I was told I was no longer his son and never to return home.'

Elena reached over to touch his arm. 'I'm sorry,' she whispered. 'I shouldn't have asked . . .'

His fingers dropped lightly over her wrist. His thumb moved back and forth across the top of her hand while he gazed at her solemnly.

She was acutely aware of his touch. She jumped to her feet. 'I must return to Savannah.' She walked quickly to the gig, then glanced over her shoulder.

With a leisurely movement, he shook out the blanket and rolled it up to fasten it behind his saddle. When he finished with everything, he lifted Elena into the gig, then climbed up beside her.

Engaged in the process of tying her bonnet beneath her chin, Elena halted and gasped, 'You can't ride back to Savannah with me!'

'I don't intend to,' he drawled. 'It's a lovely day and we have time; let's enjoy the country air.'

Elena regarded him. 'You're enjoying more than country air!'

He gazed down at her and his eyes danced mischievously. 'You think I like your company that much?'

Embarrassed, she looked away. How could he be pleasant one moment and aggravating the next, she wondered.

He laughed. 'You're quite right, Miss Blake, I'm enjoying your company more than the country air—or more than anything else right now.'

His voice changed on the last and he sounded so in earnest that she looked at him in surprise. It was impossible to discern his feelings and she shifted lest he catch her staring at him.

With an expert touch, he turned the carriage along the road away from Savannah. Elena started to protest, then bit her lip and remained silent. The horse pulled them beneath interlocking branches of tall oaks. Sparrows flitted through the leaves while greening tendrils of Spanish moss wafted with the breeze. The air smelled of spring, of lilacs, magnolias, and of freshly dug earth.

They passed rice fields where water glistened in low-lying land. She said, 'For someone turned away from home, you've done remarkably well. Four ships are a small fortune.'

His steady gaze met hers and she detected a flash of anger. He spoke cynically. 'Is that all you consider, Miss Blake? You will have one of the coldest, dullest marriages possible with Alfred Crowe.'

She turned away. 'I've told you before, it's none of your affair.' After a moment she looked at him and spoke sharply. 'I have no family. You know the lot of women. I cannot go out and take what I want as you did. If I had no wealth I would be at the mercy of others right now.'

'That still doesn't make wealth all-important.'

'Uncle Findley said nothing else will ever matter as much.'

Captain Merrick looked at her impatiently, then tugged the reins and halted the carriage. The stillness of the countryside settled over them as he spoke. 'I think it's time you realised there is something to consider in this world besides gold.'

She wished he did not have a way of regarding her so steadfastly. It made her feel as if he could see her very thoughts.

'Come here, Miss Blake,' he murmured and circled her waist to pull her to him.

She placed her hands against his chest. 'Sir! Someone might come along and you'll destroy my reputation,' she protested.

'There is little need to be concerned about your reputation,' he drawled. 'Do you know that everyone says you're as cold as ice?' His arm tightened and he ignored her words. 'I happen to know differently, Miss Blake.'

Shocked, she pushed against him. His voice deepened. 'I remember that second kiss in front of your house the other night.' His tone developed a velvety huskiness. 'You're an apt pupil at more than pistols.' His gaze shifted to her mouth.

She gasped at his boldness, yet under his piercing regard, all her protests melted away. It was difficult to get her breath, impossible to speak. She watched him draw closer until his lips merely brushed hers, then she closed her eyes.

His hand slipped behind her neck and gently exerted pressure to draw her towards him.

Elena's pulse raced; she knew she was behaving in a shocking manner, yet she was quivering in anticipation of his kiss.

'Captain . . .' she whispered.

'Lance,' he murmured and placed his mouth on hers. With tender insistence his lips sent a ripple of pleasure through her.

When the kiss deepened and became more passionate, Elena's eyes opened momentarily in surprise. Lance was watching her and she closed her eyes quickly.

She felt consumed by his kiss. His mouth was warm, insistent. He held her tightly and continued to kiss her until her arms fastened around his neck and she pressed against him. Suddenly he released her.

For a moment he studied her; his eyes were filled with curiosity, then he asked dryly, 'Did you consider money then, Miss Blake? Or did I drive that out of your thoughts for an instant?'

She blushed and shifted away from him. 'You are a rogue, Captain Merrick!'

He chuckled softly and shifted to look at her. 'It's Lance. Come on, Miss Blake, let me hear you say it.'

She gazed down at her hands. 'You know it isn't proper.'

'Hardly anything that has transpired between us since we met has been proper. I don't want to be addressed as "Captain Merrick" even one more time by you. Say my name.'

She glanced at him. 'I must return to Savannah . . .' Why was it so difficult to repeat his name? She looked down again and added, 'Lance.'

He laughed softly and tilted her chin up to face him. Elena's cheeks grew warm, but she could not turn away. He moved closer and stroked her cheek, then caught a tendril of golden hair and curled it behind her ear.

His voice was husky. 'I don't care to continue with "Miss Blake" either.'

'It's Elena,' she stated.

His blue eyes darkened. His finger traced the line of her chin while he spoke. 'Elena. That fits you. Elena, I've always known what I wanted. I had to learn early in life to make decisions and stand by them. I also learned long ago, and at quite a price, to take what I want or lose the opportunity.'

His words made no sense to her. She wondered if he was going to kiss her again and the thought sent shivers through her. The whole morning—or was it a whole day—she had not thought of time, but every moment with him had been scandalous behaviour. It was sufficient to destroy her engagement and her reputation, yet never before had she found anyone as exciting as this man.

He tugged loose the ribbons she had just fastened beneath her chin. He leaned closer and she felt certain he would hear her throbbing heartbeat.

While he slipped an arm around her waist, his voice deepened. 'Elena, I want you to be my wife.'

Shocked, she stared up at him. She could not credit what she had just heard. In dismay she blurted the first thought to come to mind, 'You know I'm engaged to Mr Crowe!'

He spoke dryly. 'Do tell me, Elena, that you are in love with Alfred Crowe.'

She placed her hands against his chest, attempting to hold him away. 'I explained to you that love has nothing to do with it.' She faced him squarely. 'Nor am I in love with you, sir, and you cannot be with me.'

It looked as if a curtain dropped across his eyes. They became cold and his jaw firmed. When he spoke there was a note of harsh determination. 'I know I want you, Elena Blake.'

He had not moved a muscle, yet in those few words there was such resolute intention that Elena's racing heartbeat threatened to become a drumroll.

With a grating huskiness he said, 'I want you—and I intend to have you.'

Even though he had not moved, her body reacted as intensely as if he had followed his proclamation with action. Her palms were damp, she felt hot and her heart pounded wildly. Her lips parted and she licked them quickly.

'You cannot . . .' she whispered.

He continued, 'I know I want you and this is the only way I'll get you. You're engaged, so I can't court you.'

'You don't even know me!' she gasped.

His arm tightened and he drew her closer. 'You are spirited, beautiful and fiery. Say you'll marry me.'

'That's impossible! Ridiculous! You know I'm promised . . .' She pushed against his chest. His arms were like steel.

He continued with a maddening, tempting persistence. 'We will be wed, Elena, that I swear. Say yes. Tell me you'll break your promise. You would do nothing but bring misery upon each other. If you didn't have a farthing Alfred would not have asked for your hand . . .'

She stiffened. 'That's an insult!'

'No. If the man cared for a beautiful young wife, he wouldn't have spent all these years a solitary bachelor.' His blue eyes were piercing. 'Tell me Alfred Crowe is deeply in love with you.'

'You know he's not!' she snapped. 'You can't be either!'

'We will deal well together, Elena. I'll make you happy. You must consent . . .'

'No! It's impossible!'

He inched closer; all her words were stopped by his mouth possessing hers. How could she argue when his exploring, demanding kiss was driving every thought out of mind?

He shifted and murmured against her ear, 'I shall go on kissing you until you yield.' His mouth crushed her soft lips. Sending bonnet and pins flying to the carriage seat, his hand locked in her hair and held her head while his arm tightened around her slender waist.

His kisses stirred such excitement in her, while his arms almost crushed the breath from her lungs. Contemplation of yielding to his demands, of marriage to this strong, hot-blooded Englishman terrified her.

At the same time . . . each kiss made her want more. He could be charming, delightfully wicked . . .

He whispered again, 'Say yes, Elena.'

All reasoning was gone, destroyed by her response to his kisses that caused her to wind her arms around his neck and return his embrace.

He raised his head. 'Say it, Elena! Will you be my wife?'

'I cannot,' she murmured dazedly. 'I've accepted Mr Crowe's ring.'

He spoke quickly. 'Return it. Far better than a lifetime of misery.'

'I will shock everyone.' Her hands were against his chest and beneath her palms she felt the vibrations of his chuckle. She pulled away slightly to look at him.

His eyes twinkled. 'You'll always shock everyone, Elena. You are far too spirited to settle down to a matronly, dull life with Alfred Crowe.' The laughter disappeared as he looked at her intently. His voice dropped to a hoarse whisper and he coaxed, 'Say yes.'

His mouth silenced the next protest and drove all others from her lips. Deftly, with unrelenting ardour he proceeded to quiet her objections, to banish all thoughts from her mind.

She twisted away momentarily and looked at him while she whispered, 'Mr Crowe wants my wealth and you want my body.'

'Aye, I want that—and more. I want your mind and your heart, Elena.'

'You cannot,' she stated, then he crushed her to him for another dizzying kiss. He kissed her until her head reeled. He drew away briefly, 'Say it! Say you will . . .'

She could not say anything. She was rocked with feelings she had never experienced. Her slender body trembled in his arms. He demanded fiercely, 'Tell me you will . . .'

'Yes.' She closed her eyes and raised her mouth. 'Yes . . . Lance.'

He leaned forward and the touch of his lips on her eyelids, her brow and her neck promised ecstasy. Finally he released her and gazed at her. 'I want you as I've never wanted any woman.'

'I hardly know you,' she murmured.

'Nor I you. It shall be a joy to learn about each other, Elena.' He picked up her hand. The diamond on her finger glittered. Carefully, Lance drew it off, turned her hand over and placed the ring in her palm.

Released from his breath-stopping embrace, a degree of sanity was returning. She gazed at him with wonder. *What have I done?* she thought. She spoke. 'I can never tell Mr Crowe.'

'Yes, you can,' he stated firmly.

Cold realisation swept through her. 'I don't want to be the wife of a sea captain and spend my life aboard ship or waiting alone while you sail around the world!'

He answered calmly, 'I intended on giving it up anyway. I'm not meant to be a seaman. I've always wanted to farm.'

Dismay changed to consternation. 'Did you do this to get my plantation?'

He threw back his head and his laughter resounded in the air.

'Oh, do hush!' She looked around as if the noise would conjure up onlookers.

His blue eyes twinkled and he spoke with amusement. 'You can give away your plantation if you choose. I have sufficient for both of us.'

'You can't mean that you actually think I would give away a plantation!' She flounced away slightly and noticed his coat. Earlier, he had tossed it casually on the seat. When he had pulled her into his arms, it had been crumpled between them. Elena reached down and smoothed it out, then looked up to see him smile. He took her hand in his and kissed her fingers lightly.

'Happy?' he asked.

She regarded him and answered. 'I'm terrified.'

His quick chuckle aggravated her and she snatched her hand away. 'Why are you laughing at me?'

'I'm not. It's at myself. You wounded my male pride.'

'I doubt that. Your arrogance is too irrepressible to hurt in the least.'

'Ah, another cruel blow!'

She gazed at him with exasperation, then had to smile. He dropped his arm around her shoulders and pulled her close to kiss her forehead.

Quickly, she turned away. 'I must make myself presentable.' She retrieved her bonnet and began to collect scattered pins. Removing a small comb from her reticule, Elena struggled to redo her hair. After a moment she glanced at him and was startled to find him facing her, one arm casually draped upon the back of the carriage seat while he watched her with interest.

She blushed and paused. 'Don't study me; it's disconcerting.'

'Good,' he stated. 'I'd hate for you to be able to ignore me.'

'That I'll never be able to do!' she muttered and placed her bonnet on her head. He leaned forward to tie the ribbons for her. She tilted her face up and could not keep from gazing at his mouth. She was conscious of each brush of his fingers.

Finally he moved away and she felt a twinge of disappointment. He picked up the reins and they started along the road.

She carefully tucked the diamond ring into her reticule, then looked at Lance. Vitality radiated from him; beneath the thin linen shirt, hard muscles bulged. The linen was as wrinkled as her bodice and his laces had come slightly unfastened to reveal a dark mat of hair on his chest.

As they approached Savannah, she looked at him. 'I think I should go on alone.'

He stopped the horse and turned to regard her. 'Would you like me to go with you to tell Alfred?'

She shook her head. 'No. That is something I should do alone,' she said, but how tempting it was to think about having him at her side when she faced Mr Crowe. She smoothed the creases in her dress.

He tilted her chin up. 'Don't fret. You and Alfred Crowe were never meant for each other.' He slipped his arm around her waist and kissed her lightly.

Elena heard hoofbeats one second before Lance slid away. A man rode around a turn and faced them.

Elena jumped farther apart from Lance and felt the blush run from her toes to her temples. It seemed as if all breath had been squeezed out of her. She wanted to faint, anything to escape the encounter, but the man raised his hat and greeted them.

It was Frederick Randall, a plantation owner. His eyes narrowed and he glanced back and forth between them rapidly. Elena could barely murmur a reply to his greeting. Lance's cool manner only increased her misery. While the two men talked, she felt dizzy and barely heard snatches of conversation.

The moment Randall rode out of sight, she clutched Lance's arm. 'Frederick Randall will ride straight to Mr Crowe and he'll challenge you to a duel!'

Lance flicked the reins and the horse commenced to trot. 'Yes,' he stated quietly.

'This will ruin my reputation!'

'I suspect that is worrying you far more than Alfred's anger.' He glanced at her. 'We must see him right away, Elena, and settle this matter. If we reach him before Randall does, perhaps there will be little turmoil over it.'

They reached a fork in the road and he turned to the left.

She looked at him quickly. 'You just took the wrong turn.'

'No,' he replied in a calm voice. 'We'll call on Alfred now and have done with this.'

She clutched Lance's arm. 'I can't! I cannot see him when I took like this. I look as if . . .' She bit her lip and blushed hotly.

'Afraid?'

'I don't want to see him when you are with me. At least, not right now.' She cried, 'You've destroyed my reputation, I'm sure!'

'Elena, people like Mary and Jason will understand and not condemn—those who act unkindly are not friends anyway.'

She sat stiffly in the carriage and rode in silence. Her enjoyment of the afternoon was shattered. Even Lance became quiet and she suspected that he was more concerned than he showed. She twisted her fingers together. *What had she done!* 'It was madness to break her promise to Alfred Crowe and give her consent to Lance Merrick. She glanced at him. He looked cool and collected, as if he had no cares whatsoever. Suppose Alfred Crowe challenged him . . . She shivered and put the thought out of mind.

Distracted, Elena ran her fingers across her brow. She looked at him again. 'You have completely unsettled my life!'

'Perhaps, Elena,' he drawled sardonically, 'you should realise that you've disturbed mine also. When I dropped anchor in Savannah's harbour, I had no intention of promising to wed.'

She remained quiet while they turned up the long drive to Galloway Hill, Alfred Crowe's plantation. Usually she enjoyed the drive beneath spreading trees until she reached the austere, but sizeable brick house.

Lance halted and jumped down to hand the reins to a stableboy. Elena felt frozen with embarrassment and fear. Thank heavens her aunt and uncle knew nothing of this turn of events!

Within moments Lance climbed back into the gig and took the reins to head down the drive for the road.

'He's in Savannah,' he stated.

'Oh, no!' Worriedly, she squeezed her fingers together. By the time they would reach Savannah, it would be late afternoon.

A muscle worked in Lance's jaw and he glanced at her sharply. 'Now don't start weeping,' he stated quietly.

'I ought to draw that pistol and put a ball right through your heart!' Elena snapped.

Suddenly stiffness left his shoulders and his mouth curled in a wicked grin that made her even angrier. 'That, my dear, is exactly one of the reasons I want you for my wife. I'll not wed a simpering miss.'

Elena cared not a trifle for his rambling conversation. She tossed her head and shifted away from him.

Lance kept the horse at a trot as much as possible and finally they reached Savannah. As they rode down Bull Street, Elena gazed blankly at houses graced by ornamental ironwork on balconies and stairs. They passed Johnson Square and rounded a corner to head for her house.

Elena drew a sharp breath and clutched Lance's arm as she straightened in terror.

CHAPTER
THREE

ALFRED Crowe's black carriage was in front of Elena's house. Lance halted the gig, shrugged into his coat and jumped down. 'Wait just a minute, Elena,' he instructed before heading for Alfred's carriage to speak to the coachman.

She watched him and thought he looked little changed from when she had met him in the morning. Over a dozen times she had smoothed her rumpled dress and knew how dishevelled she appeared.

Lance returned to help her out of the carriage. 'Alfred's inside.'

'Oh, Lance, I can't face him!'

'Yes, you can.' He held her arm lightly and they started towards the door. He spoke softly. 'Elena, you haven't committed a crime—you both will be better for this. Neither of you would have been happy.' They were half-way along the brick walk when the front door flew open and a red-faced Alfred Crowe burst forth. He took the steps two at a time, marched resolutely up to them and regarded Elena with shaking rage.

'You trollop!'

Instantly Lance's hand shot out and he snatched Alfred Crowe's shirt-front. 'She doesn't deserve that! Apologise, Crowe!'

'You swine!' he snapped. 'Unhand me at once!'

'Like hell! Apologise!'

With a vicious swing, Alfred Crowe backhanded Lance and snarled, 'I demand satisfaction!'

Lance tightened his fist and lifted Alfred Crowe until

only the tips of his boots touched the ground. Elena wrung her hands and cried, 'Please, Lance, unhand Mr Crowe. Let me give him his ring.'

Lance let out his breath. He released Alfred Crowe and said, 'I'll send my second to call.'

Elena held out the diamond ring.

Alfred Crowe snatched it and marched past them to climb into his carriage. It began to move down the street; the horses' hoofs clattered against the bricks.

Elena looked up at Lance whose fists were still clenched. 'Suppose he kills you,' she whispered.

He turned to gaze at her. 'Would you care?'

'Of course, I'd care,' she stated impatiently. 'I just promised to marry you. You've ruined my reputation . . .' Trembling swept through her.

He regarded her sombrely. 'Elena, under the circumstances, I think we should be wed as soon as possible. It will put an end to malicious gossip.'

'How could you have done this to me!'

'I never intended for it to be this way,' his voice hardened, 'but those kisses were not received unwillingly or through force.'

'Of all the nerve, Lance Merrick!' she stated in a low voice which was filled with fury. She reached up and slapped his cheek, then whirled to dash into the house.

With his usual aloof expression, Hadley opened the door and greeted her as if she had returned from an afternoon stroll. Elena rushed past him for her room, tears streaming down her cheeks as she went upstairs. In the hall she encountered Dorset and her spirits plummeted at the maid's frowning countenance.

'Miss Elena! What have you done?'

'Dorset, please fetch supper to my room. I'm hungry, but I don't feel well enough to eat downstairs.'

'Aye, Ma'am,' Dorset replied.

Elena reached her room and threw herself across the bed to sob. She should not have slapped Lance. What he had said had been true. She did like his kisses, but why did Frederick Randall have to run straight to Mr Crowe? Alfred Crowe's terrible words rang in her ears. At the thought that he might kill Lance a fresh burst of tears came forth.

A knock sounded and Dorset entered with a tray. She placed it on a small writing-desk and turned to face Elena.

Elena's fingers were squeezed together so tightly it was painful. She took a deep breath and said, 'Dorset, I'm going to wed Captain Merrick.'

The maid gasped and pressed her hand to her heart. 'You cannot, Ma'am! You are promised to Mr Crowe!'

Elena gazed at Dorset defiantly. 'Mr Crowe wouldn't wed me now anyway.'

'What have you done?' Dorset's bushy brown brows came together in a frown.

'Dorset, don't scold. Captain Merrick is a good man.'

'But a sea captain . . .'

Elena interrupted, 'He's the son of an English gentleman and he intends to settle and farm.'

'Saints preserve!' Dorset clutched her forehead. 'Ye cannot know the man at all. He could be a brigand, a pirate . . .'

'No. The Jacksons are good friends of his and you know they wouldn't associate with brigands.'

'Hmmpf. 'Tis a sorry mess you've made.'

'We will wed soon,' Elena rose and moved to the dinner tray. She wished Dorset's brown eyes would not gaze at her so accusingly.

'No one in Savannah will speak to you.' When Elena did not answer, Dorset added, 'You do not look over-joyed, Ma'am.'

Elena glanced at her. She regretted the way the day had gone, but deep inside knowledge was growing that she was not sorry that her engagement to Alfred Crowe was broken. She said, 'Dorset, I'm ready to eat now.'

The maid drew herself up and left the room grumbling, her words barely discernible except Elena heard, 'disgrace'. As soon as the door closed, Elena gazed down at the tray of steaming, brown pork chops, turnips and golden corn-bread. Even though she had not eaten since breakfast, all appetite had vanished.

She moved to the window and looked outside. It would be a relief to go to the plantation and stay. When Aunt Agnes had become ill, Elena's uncle had built the home in Savannah. After his illness Elena preferred to stay in town rather than on the plantation, but now it would be a relief to escape the scandal.

A knock sounded and Elena started to send Dorset away when she heard a soft voice.

'Elena . . .' Mary Jackson stepped inside.

'Mary, thank goodness you're here!' Elena crossed the room and hugged her friend.

Looking at Elena, Mary said, 'Lance has been over to talk to Jason. Jason will be his second.'

'Oh, no! I don't want Jason drawn into this.'

Mary spoke quietly. 'He's willing to. Lance would do the same for him.'

Elena looked at her with curiosity. 'Come sit down, Mary. How did Jason get to know Lance?'

Mary saw the dinner tray. 'Elena, you must eat. I'll stay, but you eat your dinner.'

While Elena moved to the desk, Mary sat in a rocker and talked. 'They knew each other in England. Jason never mentions his family, but there were four sons and he was the youngest, so Jason was the last in line to inherit. He didn't get along well with his father—which may be one reason he was such close friends with Lance. They are also close in age. Lance is twenty-nine, just two years younger than Jason. Anyway, Jason came here to live when he was only twenty-one.'

Elena thought of Jason, tall, red-headed and fair-skinned, who printed Savannah's newspaper and handled it with quiet competence. 'I can't bear them to duel because of me,' she whispered.

'Jason is willing,' Mary replied quietly. 'He has never cared for Mr Crowe since the man tried to cheat him once in business dealings.'

Elena looked up in surprise. 'Mary, you never told me that!'

'I saw no reason to, but I'm so happy you'll wed Lance. I just knew you would like him.'

Elena frowned. 'Is that why you seated me next to him at your party?'

Mary smiled and nodded. 'I didn't know you had already met him.'

Elena put down her fork. She could not eat another bite. She placed her head in her hands. 'Mary, you and Jason will be the only people in Savannah who will speak to me!'

'Hardly, Elena. There are many people here who like both you and Lance. Gossip will end once you're married. Lance said the wedding will take place in two weeks.'

Elena straightened and gazed at Mary in exasperation. 'He didn't discuss any date with me!'

'He will,' Mary answered calmly and rose. 'I must get home, but I had to come and see you. I can tell Dorset is upset, but she'll take good care of you. Come over in the morning and we'll start your wedding dress.'

'Mary, when is the duel?'

'Day after tomorrow at dawn. It'll be a quarter mile out on the river road.'

'Thank you for coming.' Elena followed her friend downstairs to the door. After Mary's departure Elena returned to her room. She felt only slightly better. She worried about people's feelings and about the coming duel. It would be dreadful enough if Alfred Crowe were killed—unthinkable if it were Lance. She could not bear to consider it and know that she was the cause.

She spent a sleepless night and rose early to dress in a sedate dark blue poplin with long sleeves and a white, lace-trimmed high neck. Throwing a shawl around her shoulders and placing a bonnet on her curls, Elena gathered parasol and gloves and headed for the Jacksons'. Their home was around the corner and she preferred to walk rather than take a carriage, but as soon as she saw someone approaching, she wished she had ridden in a carriage.

Mrs Hartman and Mrs Johnson drew abreast, but neither woman returned Elena's greeting. Instead, they looked away and continued their conversation while they passed her.

Elena bit her lips and flushed with embarrassment. It hurt to be snubbed and she wondered if she would forever be ostracised. She reached the Jacksons' wrought iron gate and pushed it open to run up the steps to the door.

Jason had gone to the shop, but Mary greeted her warmly and urged her to come in. Later, Mary accompanied her to purchase lace and satin for a wedding dress. People spoke, but Elena knew it was because Mary Jackson was at her side.

After eating cold sliced ham and hot biscuits with plum jelly, Elena told Mary she must return home. She pulled the shawl around her shoulders as she started along the brick walk away from the Jacksons'.

She heard hoofbeats behind her and stiffened, dreading any encounter, then Lance's voice called, 'Elena! Wait a minute . . .'

She looked around as he halted and motioned to her. 'Come on and get in.'

'I'm almost home,' she protested.

'Come on.'

Elena saw another carriage approaching and decided she would be less conspicuous if she rode with him. She hurried to climb in and sit down. With a glance at his finely tailored brown coat and leather breeches, she decided he did not look as if he had spent a sleepless night. She said, 'You don't appear to have a care in the world!'

He smiled and glanced at her. 'If looks were damaging, I'm afraid I'd be gone now.'

She raised her chin and stared ahead. 'Well, you've caused me no end of trouble. No one will speak to me . . .'

He looked at her sharply. 'Do you mean that?'

'Of course I mean it! Will men speak to you?' The instant she uttered the words, bitterness filled her. 'Of course they will,' she answered her own question. 'This scandal will only make you look more dashing and exciting . . .'

'Elena . . .' He took her hand in his. His voice was filled with such tenderness that she felt all her anger and hurt fade away.

'Elena, love, this will all end. We'll wed soon and then the gossip will cease.'

She exclaimed, 'Lance, you passed my house!'

'Yes. Elena, the day is beautiful; let's go for a ride.'

'I can't!' she cried.

He looked at her. 'Why not? You have nothing more to lose. All Savannah has gossiped about our activities. A carriage ride on a pretty day won't make things worse.'

She bit her lip and stared at him. He reached out and drew her closer, then kissed her lightly. His voice was soft. 'I'm sorry someone ignored you.'

After the strain of the past hours, his kindness and attention were too much. Hot tears sprang to her eyes and Elena placed her head against his shoulder.

'Everything is . . . so terrible!' she sobbed.

'Shh, love. No, it's not terrible. We'll be wed soon, Elena.'

She sobbed harder. Dimly she realised they were

moving at a brisker pace. He had urged the horses to a trot and soon they were away from residences and riding along the bluff overlooking the harbour. The horses' hoofs rang against the grey cobblestones which had been brought from England.

Finally they were out of Savannah. Lance halted the carriage and turned to take her into his arms. He held her close and patted her shoulder.

Elena grew quiet, then she shifted and gazed up at him. 'This is dreadful,' she whispered.

When he looked down questioningly, she explained, 'You said you don't like simpering misses . . .'

She felt the rumble in his chest when he chuckled. He tilted her face up and wiped away a tear with his finger. 'You aren't simpering and you've had sufficient cause to stir a tear or two. Let me see you smile.'

'I can't! Lance, I can't bear the thought of a duel because of me.'

'Forget it, Elena. It's not the first time for either Alfred or me.'

She shuddered. 'Duelling is barbaric.'

'I'll not kill Alfred nor will he kill me. The first to draw blood will settle the matter.'

She studied him and doubted his words. 'Mr Crowe looked angry enough to shoot to kill. For that matter— you did also.'

'Elena, don't concern yourself with it.'

'And there's Jason, who'll be your second. Jason is so mild-tempered.

Lance stated quietly. 'Jason is a peaceful man who loves his wife and his books, but he's also a deadly shot.'

'Jason?'

'Yes. He'll not be involved in any shooting anyway. Now, for the next hour let's hear no more about the duel.'

She sighed and promised, 'All right. I'll try, but it's difficult to forget.'

He turned and picked up the reins. 'When we're wed, I want to take you on the *Sea Hawk* for a wedding trip.'

She glanced at him. 'Are all of your ships here now?'

'Aye, for the time being. It's safer to stay together.'

'Are any of them pirate ships?'

He laughed. 'No, Elena. I earn quite a respectable living now. My pirating days are over, I pray. I intend to sell two ships and purchase sufficient land to establish a plantation. I'll keep the other ships active. The British may not welcome me, but they're eager for my ships to arrive. I do a good trade in cotton, rum and tobacco and as long as I stay away from British waters or England, all is fine. Tariffs are high on British goods coming into America, but I can do a satisfactory business. Factories are springing up all the time as more and more goods are produced here.' He glanced around. 'This country is growing, Elena, and I want to grow with it.'

'You want to settle and raise tobacco?' she asked.

'No,' he replied. 'The Georgia tutor with his invention has revolutionised cotton production.'

Elena regarded him and decided she had never seen such blue eyes and long black lashes. 'I have heard talk of Mr Whitney's cotton engine.'

Lance looked past her at a furrowed field. 'Along the coast is "sea-island cotton". It's not too difficult to separate by hand, but away from the coast you have upland cotton with short fibres. By hand it took a day, Elena, to get a pound. With this cotton *gin* a man can produce more than fifty pounds a day.' He looked down at her. 'That's if the machine is hand-driven. If run by motor, it can produce one thousand pounds a day. Mills are springing up in the north and buying cotton.' He faced the road. 'The market is good in England. Cotton is the crop I want, Elena.'

She glanced at him. All his talk about cotton was of little concern to her. 'Lance, is Paris really a wicked city? I hear tales about it . . .'

He laughed and touched her chin lightly with his finger. 'Someday I will take you to see for yourself.'

Following a narrow, dusty road as it meandered beneath the oaks, with their graceful long tresses of Spanish moss, they moved at a leisurely pace while Lance related his adventures in Calais. He braced his booted foot beneath the seat of the carriage. The walnut box with the duelling pistols was on the floor of the carriage. Warm sunshine had caused Lance to peel off his coat, revealing rippling muscles across his back beneath a white cambric shirt. Its full sleeves were fastened around bony wrists above his strong brown fingers.

For the first time since they had encountered Frederick Randall, Elena began to relax.

Lance gazed around and remarked, 'This is a good land, Elena. This new President, Thomas Jefferson, is interested in development. A Virginian, he'll have the needs of southern planters in his heart.' He looked down at her. 'Have you ever been north?'

When she shook her head, he continued, 'I want you to see Virginia. We might settle there.'

She gazed at him with surprise. 'You don't want to stay in Savannah?'

He shrugged and studied her. 'Not necessarily. Would you mind leaving?'

'You really don't want my plantation, do you?'

He shook his head. 'No. If you like, you can put it up for sale tomorrow. The money from it will be yours—unless you're sentimental about it. We can find someone to run it if you'd rather, then you can have the income from it.'

'I don't mind selling it,' she replied.

He glanced at her. 'Weren't you happy there?'

Elena placed a blue reticule in her lap and smoothed the poplin skirt. 'Yes, but I don't mind parting with it. Aunt Agnes took care of me, but . . . I don't think she ever really wanted me.' Elena was aware of Lance watching her and she looked down at her hands. 'That is why . . .' She paused a moment. It was difficult to express feelings she had never put into words before. 'That's why there is a special feeling between Dorset and me—she is more than a servant. She brought me here from England. She has no family.' The next words were spoken quickly. 'In a way she was more a mother to me than Aunt Agnes. Also, I shared common interests with Uncle Findley. After I was older he began to confide his concerns about the plantation.' She looked up to find Lance's blue eyes intently on her.

He reached over to take her hand in his. 'We'll sell that plantation and you can have the money,' he stated quietly.

'Lance, after we wed I want Dorset to remain with me.'

'Of course,' he replied easily. 'Bring anyone you want.'

'Hadley is special too. Years ago he lost his wife and son; when I was young, he was so good to me.' She glanced at him in speculation. 'Lance, even Mr Crowe made no such offer to me—to sell my plantation and give me the proceeds. You must be very wealthy.'

He grinned. 'Thank goodness. I would never get your consideration, much less consent, if I weren't.' The words were spoken lightly, yet she detected a cynical tone in his voice.

She turned away and gazed at tall pines. After a moment she said, 'Perhaps, Lance, if you hadn't spent so much time aboard ship, you would have found a girl to wed sooner.'

He smiled. 'I haven't spent that much time at sea, Elena. There are women in every port.'

'You're so handsome. I should think there would be many women eager to wed you.'

The corners of his mouth twitched. 'Why, thank you, Elena. I'm happy to know that you find me handsome!'

She blushed. 'Do not make so much of it. You are also arrogant beyond the pale.'

He looked down at her and spoke sardonically. 'I had no inclination for a wedded state until yesterday.'

'How can you de . . .' Her words were broken off as a scream rent the air. Lance's eyes narrowed and he flicked the reins to urge the horse to a gallop in the direction of the noise. Another scream sounded, a high wail which made Elena grow cold.

They rounded a bend and in a grassy stretch beyond a copse of trees saw a buggy pulled off the road. In the seat of the buggy a girl struggled against a scantily-clad man. The man looked up, saw them approaching and began quickly to replace his clothing.

They drew alongside the buggy. Lance reined and leapt from the carriage.

A girl huddled in the buggy. Great racking sobs caused her to shake violently. The man faced them and Elena recognised Mr Kaufman, a successful lumber dealer who had moved to Savannah two years earlier.

'Merrick, see here!' he blustered angrily.

Lance swore violently. He reached up and his brown fingers closed on Horatio Kaufman's rumpled shirt-front. Muscles bunched in Lance's arm as he snatched the man out of the carriage. He slammed his fist into Kaufman's jaw.

While the men fought, Elena scrambled into the buggy to comfort the hysterical girl. She put her arm around the girl's thin shoulders, then watched the men, her heart pounded in fear.

Lance hit Kaufman a resounding blow. He staggered back against the carriage, then kicked Lance. 'Get out of here, Merrick! 'Tis none of your affair! Leave me alone or I'll have you run out of Savannah forever.'

Lance faced him and swore softly. 'I take the girl with me, Kaufman.'

'You damned rascal! Don't you touch her.' His fists

were raised as he moved warily in front of Lance. Kaufman's pale eyes glanced at Elena. He sneered. 'You have your own doxy. Take her . . .'

With startling swiftness Lance moved forward. There was a sound of bone on bone as his knuckles cracked against Kaufman's jaw. Kaufman reeled backwards, then lunged at Lance.

Swiftly jabbing with his right fist, he followed in a solid blow with his left. It sent Lance crashing into his carriage.

Elena drew a sharp breath and had to bite her lip to keep from screaming. A trickle of red showed on Lance's chin. His lip was cut and his cheekbone was scraped. Dark hair curled in disarray over his forehead.

Horatio Kaufman snarled, 'I'm telling you, Merrick, leave me alone!'

Lance's fist shot into Kaufman's middle. The man exhaled loudly and doubled over. He barrelled forward and ploughed into Lance; they both toppled to the ground.

Elena shook with fright. The girl trembled so violently her teeth chattered. Her thin bones were angular against a coarse white cotton dress. The flimsy material was torn and ripped. With her head in her hands she sobbed in a high, keening wail that could not drown out the noise of flesh striking flesh or snorts of effort from the men. Elena felt on the edge of hysterics too. There was nothing she could do to aid Lance, and it was dreadful to watch Kaufman pummel him with his fists.

Suddenly Lance hit Kaufman with a blow which made a crack like a limb snapping. He staggered away, then stumbled against his carriage and reached inside.

Elena saw his hands and gasped. She lunged to grab his arm and he slapped her viciously.

With a cry she fell back into the carriage. Horatio Kaufman spun around and snapped, 'All right, you damned rogue, I'll teach you to step in where you're told not to.'

Lance had moved to his carriage to get his pistol, but he halted and remained motionless as he faced Horatio Kaufman's weapon. Silver flashed in the sunlight as Horatio Kaufman pointed his flintlock at Lance's heart.

CHAPTER
FOUR

SHEER terror enveloped Elena. She glanced around desperately and, noticing the reticule still dangling from her wrist, she yanked it off. She flung her reticule at Kaufman. It struck his head in a harmless blow, but for a moment it distracted him.

Lance reached over and retrieved his pistol from beneath the carriage seat.

Horatio Kaufman fired at Lance.

Elena felt as if she would faint. She clutched the sides of the carriage and stared at Lance. He remained standing. He raised his arm and returned fire.

The weapons were deafening in the stillness.

While a dark stain spread across his chest, Horatio Kaufman collapsed.

Elena began to scramble down out of the carriage. When Lance reached her, she whispered, 'She's only a child. I think she's hurt badly.'

Lance stated, 'We must get her away from here. Get in the carriage, Elena. I'll bring the girl.' He knelt and placed his hand against Kaufman's throat, then straightened and climbed into the carriage to lift the girl into his arms. She cried out once as she wrapped thin arms around his neck. He crossed to get into his carriage and place the girl between them.

Elena put her arms around the girl's shoulders and attempted to brush straggles of brown hair from the tear-streaked face.

She looked over the girl's head and spoke. 'Lance, her face is bruised and her lip is cut.'

He swore softly and reached around to pick up his coat and place it over the girl's shoulders. Next, he withdrew a cambric handkerchief and dabbed gently at her lip, then turned to pick up the reins.

Elena held the lace on her sleeve and touched his jaw. 'You need to do the same for yourself. Are you hurt badly?'

He shook his head and pressed his sleeve against a cut. 'No, I'm all right. I'll take her to your house, Elena, and I'll send for a surgeon from my ship. Keep this quiet. There's no reason to involve you or the girl. I'll go to the authorities and tell them what happened, but I won't reveal her whereabouts and you're not to either. I'll say she fled when we arrived.' His brow furrowed as he stated, 'These things can get ugly and I don't want you involved.'

She gazed up at him silently and thought how quickly he could change from teasing arrogance to protective kindness.

When they reached Elena's house, Lance jumped down and carried the girl inside. An astounded Hadley opened the door and stepped out of the way.

Lance paused to order, 'Hadley, get to my ship, the *Sea Hawk*, and fetch the surgeon, Dr Crown. Don't tell anyone what you've seen.'

'Aye, Captain Merrick.'

Lance looked at Elena. 'Where may I take her?'

'This way,' she replied and moved ahead to climb the stairs. They reached a bed chamber at the end of the hall. Elena turned down the bed, then stepped back while Lance gently laid the girl on clean white sheets. He straightened and brushed her hair from her eyes.

'That animal!' he murmured. 'She is a mere babe.' He looked at Elena, and she knew it was just as well Kaufman had died, for Lance would have killed him under any conditions. He asked, 'Can we get some heated water? I'll sponge her face.'

'Certainly,' she answered and left to find Dorset. She returned to see Lance sitting beside the girl holding her hand. His shirt sleeves were turned back against his dark arms. A cover was spread over the girl.

Elena moved to the opposite side of the bed and looked down. The girl's wide grey eyes were filled with fear. Her brown hair was in a wild tangle. Lance looked at Elena and stated, 'Her name is Madeline Adams, and she is William Bacon's bond servant. He gave her to Kaufman for the afternoon.'

'Oh, no!' Elena gasped.

Madeline closed her eyes and tears coursed down her cheeks. Lance lifted a corner of the coverlet and wiped them away. Behind him, Dorset entered with a tea-kettle. She crossed to the washstand to fill a pitcher and bowl.

Lance rose and took a cloth from Dorset, squeezed hot water through it, then returned to the bedside to sponge Madeline's face and hands.

A bruise darkened her cheek, skin around one eye was red and her lip had become puffed. Lance asked, 'Madeline, has William Bacon ever harmed you? Has he ever touched you like this?'

Elena stared at Lance. She had never heard him speak with such gentleness. When Madeline squeezed her eyes closed and began to cry, Elena whispered, 'Don't ask her about it now.'

Lance swore softly. 'There's no need to ask more.'

Elena gazed at him with worry. 'If you kill him, you'll hang,' she stated.

Lance looked up and his blue eyes were points of ice. 'Not if it's in a duel, Elena. I'll take care of the other matter first, but then I intend to challenge Bacon.'

'You're already facing a duel with Mr Crowe!'

He shrugged. 'That is an affair of honour—this is different, but both must be done.'

Dorset rapped softly before she opened the door to

admit a tall man carrying a black bag. Lance rose to introduce Dr John Crown. Elena gazed up at a fair-haired man; he spoke, then turned to Madeline.

Lance's voice was soft as he said, 'Madeline, this is Dr Crown. He'll care for you.' Leaving Dr Crown in charge, he turned away and motioned to Elena.

Once in the hall, Lance faced her and said, 'I'll report Kaufman's demise, then I intend to call on Bacon. Remember what I instructed. Don't let it be known that Madeline is here. I'll say she ran away; never mention that you were with me. As soon as possible, I'll move her to one of my ships. I can find a home where the child will have proper care.' He took Elena's hands. 'Can you give John a room if necessary? He'll bring no trouble to you.'

'Of course. Lance, they may arrest you.'

His eyes narrowed and he regarded her. 'Could it be, Elena, that you're interested in my welfare?'

She blushed. 'I don't want to see you hanged for doing a good deed.'

He laughed. 'I have no intention of hanging.' After brushing her cheek lightly with his lips, Lance hurried down the steps. She moved to the wooden banister and looked down at his dark hair until Hadley opened the door and Lance disappeared outside.

Hours passed slowly. Sleep was impossible; within a short time Lance would duel Mr Crowe. Elena paced the floor and wondered where Lance was and what he was doing.

During the night John Crown decided it would be safer to move Madeline to the ship before the light of dawn. Elena agreed, but when the two had departed under Hadley's care, a grim foreboding filled Elena. With each second, worry about the duel increased.

Finally she could stand no more. With shaking hands she dressed quickly in the dark blue poplin. Flinging a black cape over her shoulders, she pulled its hood around her face and slipped downstairs.

Soon it would be dawn and she felt certain Mary and Jason would be readying for the duel. She closed her front door and ran along the brick walk towards the Jacksons' house.

Just as she had suspected, they were up and dressed. Mary held open the door and Elena apologised for arriving at such an hour. She asked, 'Is Lance here?'

Behind her, Jason Jackson entered the room. The lanky red-headed man stood in the dimly-lit room and answered, 'No, Miss Blake, he's not here.'

She looked at his sombre countenance, then at Mary's worried brown eyes. 'Something's happened to him.'

Jason moved to the desk to open it and produce a brace of pistols. He glanced at Elena. 'Lance has been arrested.'

'Impossible!' Elena gasped.

'There will be a hearing in the morning—or rather in a few hours now,' Jason stated while he turned a flintlock in his hands.

'The duel! You can't fight this duel!' Elena cried.

He glanced at her. 'It's time to go.'

Elena grasped his arm when he reached the door. 'Jason, I can't bear this! I am the cause and I'll not have you fighting for me!'

With deliberation he unfastened her cold fingers from his arm. He looked over her head at his wife. 'I must go. I'm glad to do this—it will settle an old score. Alfred Crowe cheated me once and I let Mary talk me out of challenging him on it. He has laughed at me since over the matter. This will put an end to that.'

He moved to his wife and tilted her chin upwards while he kissed her briefly. 'I'll be home soon, Mary.'

He took a cloak from a peg and placed a wide-brimmed hat on his head, then stepped outside. The moment the door closed behind him, Mary and Elena looked at each other. Elena cried, 'Mary, I've caused this!'

'Jason is doing what he thinks he must do.'

Elena looked at the darkness outside the window. 'It'll be dawn shortly.' She gazed at her friend. 'I can't wait here. I'm going to ride out there.'

'I'll come too.' Mary Jackson gathered up cape and gloves, blew out candles, then stepped outside with Elena. Deciding they would draw less attention if they went on horseback instead of riding in a carriage, they aroused Perkins and asked him to saddle two horses.

As the horses' hoofs clattered against cobblestones, streaks of dawn lightened the morning. A grey swirling mist gave an ethereal quality to purple clusters of wisteria, red jasmine and camellias. They rode past squares which alternated like a chess-board with blocks of houses and shops. Laid out long ago by General Oglethorpe, Elena knew the open squares served as camp-ground for militia in times of military trouble, but this morning they were parks filled with blooming shrubs and flowers.

Nearing the duelling site, they halted far enough away to be hidden from view. Both women dismounted and tethered the horses, then Elena looked at Mary. 'Please, wait here. You mustn't watch.'

'I have to,' Mary whispered.

Treading quietly on leaves and twigs wet with moisture from fog, they moved between tall trees. Through the mist they saw men readying for a confrontation. Elena felt chilled to the bone. She could not bear to watch, and she could not look away.

Within minutes it commenced. Paces were counted as the men, backs to each other, stepped away until the signal was given to turn and fire.

CHAPTER
FIVE

Elena held her breath and squeezed Mary's fingers. Both men turned and took aim. Alfred Crowe fired.

The blast was loud; a puff of smoke rose from the pistol. Jason did not move.

Suddenly Alfred Crowe turned and fled. Another shot rang out and Jason's weapon smoked.

Yelping, Alfred Crowe jumped into the air. He clutched the seat of his breeches and fell to the ground while the physician and his second rushed to him.

Elena threw her hands over her mouth to hold back a giggle. She did not know whether the laughter was from relief that neither man was killed or from the ludicrous wound inflicted upon Alfred Crowe. She was overwhelmingly thankful it was done and Jason was unharmed.

When Elena finally reached home and returned to her room, she stretched on the bed and fell asleep. By the time she aroused, she was horrified to discover it was mid-morning. Immediately, Elena summoned Dorset and hurried to dress to visit Lance.

Within the hour, Elena, clad in a green silk dress with a striped spencer, was driven to the building which housed both court-house and jail. She was led to a small, bare room and asked to wait while a guard fetched Lance.

He was in the same rumpled white shirt and leather breeches as when he had bid her farewell; on his chin was a stubble of whiskers, but his teeth flashed as he smiled at her.

'Lance!' She rushed towards him, then halted with embarrassment.

He laughed and reached out to catch her wrist and narrow the remaining space. 'Do not stop, Elena. Give me the hug you intended.' His arms wrapped around her and he tilted her chin to raise her lips to his.

For an instant she forgot the jail, his arrest, and her problems. Kissing him always produced the most giddying effect. He released her and she gazed at him with wide eyes.

'Goddammit! I think I am making headway,' he murmured with amusement, but his eyes regarded her intently.

'Oh, Lance!' She lowered her head to hide the blush she knew he would see. 'It's dreadful you're here!'

'Elena, you are concerned for my welfare!'

She looked at him and saw a wicked grin. 'You're teasing, Lance, but this is a serious matter.'

He sobered and placed his hands on her shoulders.

'I've had a hearing. Trial commences tomorrow. I did no more than defend myself and I'll be easily exonerated. Don't fret.'

'If only I could testify for you, Lance. I witnessed all of it.'

He smiled. 'I won't allow you to get involved, Elena. Nor do I want Madeline involved.' His voice dropped to a whisper. 'If they find her, they'll return her to Bacon, and I have no intention of that. Before I was arrested, I challenged him. When I'm released, the first thing I'll do is tend to the duel.'

'Oh, no!' she gasped and once again received a swift, probing glance.

He said, 'Speaking of duels—you haven't asked about Jason.'

'I didn't ask because I know. Mary and I rode out there and watched.'

'The devil!' He grinned. 'Jason didn't know that?'

She shook her head. 'No, we left as soon as Mr Crowe received his injury.'

Lance chuckled. 'Merely a flesh wound, but it gave Jason satisfaction. It will put an end forever to Alfred Crowe's needling remarks.' He sobered and inquired, 'How's Madeline?'

Elena told him, 'John Crown took her to the *Sea Hawk*. Lance, the girl is only fifteen.' She shivered and looked up. 'You feel I'm too concerned with gold, but look at Madeline. A woman has no rights, as you well know, but you'll never understand because you're a man. My wealth gives me the only freedom I can ever have; if I didn't possess it, I'd be as Madeline is—at the mercy of others.'

Solemnly, he gazed at her and traced his finger along her cheek. His blue eyes were intense. 'I want you, Elena, because you're not simpering and fearful. In many ways you're as tough as I am . . .'

Exasperated at his ridiculous statement, she exclaimed, 'Lance, that's absurd!'

'Aye, you are more than you realise.' He grinned. 'How many young misses would dare to interfere with an armed man? You saved my life by throwing your reticule at Horatio Kaufman.' He tilted her face upwards. His voice dropped. 'Also, I'm certain you have a tender warm heart and you're a hot-blooded wench . . .'

'Lance Merrick!' With exasperation she tossed her head. 'It's time I departed.'

He laughed and caught her arm as she started to turn away. 'Come here, Elena.'

A knock interrupted him. The door opened and the guard told Elena she would have to leave, then he stepped outside again.

She looked up at Lance's mocking eyes. 'Lance Merrick, you are a rogue!' Even though she was irritated with him, Lance seemed too filled with vitality to be locked away in a small room. Impulsively, she stood on tiptoe to brush his cheek with a kiss. His beard was rough; the stubble made her lips tingle.

She turned away, but was aware of his eyes following her.

With a sense of unreality the next morning Elena dressed in dark blue silk and went to the court-house for Lance's trial. She mounted steps and entered a wide hall. Men milled around and she was thankful she had asked Hadley and Dorset to accompany her. They entered a large room which held rows of benches for observers.

The instant Lance appeared, his gaze met hers. He looked calm, and someone had furnished him a change of clothing. In spite of bruises on his cheek and jaw, how elegant he was! Elena's heart quickened as she took in his snowy cravat and deep blue coat. Before he turned his back to be seated, he glanced at her and winked.

Warmth coursed through her. She hoped this would be a short business; she did not care for the courtroom in the least and would be immensely relieved when Lance could join her.

At his side, the attorney Matthew Conway was a contrast. Short, blond and fair-skinned, he had a quick wit and an agile mind. Elena had known him since childhood and she felt he was as good a lawyer as Lance could hope to find in Savannah. She shifted and glanced around the room.

Morning sunlight streamed through high windows and revealed specks of dust across the pine-planked floor. With the exception of Dorset and herself, the spectators were male and Elena was thankful she had selected a less conspicuous seat at the back of the room.

She looked up to see Jason Jackson slip on to the bench beside her. He reached over and squeezed her hand; she leaned close to whisper, 'Thank you for coming.'

'Glad to,' he answered. She watched William Bacon enter and sit at the front. Elena decided not all the finery in the world could make the man look appealing. While his clothing was as elegant as Lance Merrick's, William Bacon's squat body, thick neck and full fat lips made Elena shudder. All of Savannah knew of his temper and Elena pitied Madeline for having to spend even one hour as his bond servant.

She heard booted feet and observed a giant of a man stride down the aisle. Beneath a floppy hat his dark hair was braided into plaits which stood out all over his head in an odd contrast to a full bushy beard and moustache. She leaned close to Jason. 'I'd hate to encounter him in the dark. Who is that?'

Jason whispered that he did not know while Elena noticed that the man's shoulders were as broad as Lance's and he was fully two inches taller. A scar ran across his forehead. He sat down on the second bench from the front.

Lance sat in the box with his back to spectators, yet when the man reached a seat, Lance turned to look at him. There was not a flicker of change in his features, but Elena suddenly felt certain Lance knew the man.

Her guess was confirmed when the man grinned widely at Lance. Lance's mouth curled in a mocking smile, then he faced the front.

Elena wondered who the man could be and why he was present. From the sardonic expression on Lance's face, she did not think the man was one of Lance's seamen. She forgot about it as John Crown came in, accompanied by six swarthy men. She guessed all were from the *Sea Hawk* or one of Lance's ships. While Elena's tension mounted, Judge Myer Lindsay entered and the trial commenced.

The solemn-faced judge intoned the words, 'People versus Edward Lancelot Pennington Merrick. The charge: murder.' A chill ran through Elena at the finality of the accusation.

A plea of 'not guilty by reason of self-defence' was

entered by Matthew Conway. The first witness summoned was William Bacon. As his testimony fell upon the ears of the Court, his words made Madeline Adams appear a dishonest, immoral wench. Elena was enraged by the falsehoods. She clenched her fists in her lap and whispered to Jason, 'I know his words are untrue!' To hear Bacon talk, he had seen to the girl's welfare and generously cared for her.

The attorney asked if Madeline Adams had known Captain Merrick. William Bacon cleared his throat and replied, 'Yes.' His pale eyes shifted and he looked quickly at the attorney, then gazed into space while he spoke. 'The girl has known Captain Merrick since his second night in port. Both Horatio and Captain Merrick were attracted to her. Merrick threatened to kill Kaufman . . .'

Elena saw Lance straighten. Matthew Conway jumped to his feet. 'Objection! This man is lying!'

The spectators rose. A shout was heard from one of Lance's men, then several cries rang out. Elena could not see for the men standing in front of her. She jumped to her feet beside Jason and stood on tiptoe in an attempt to get a view of Lance.

The courtroom was brought to order by a pounding gavel, then Judge Lindsay sternly admonished the attorneys.

Matthew Conway's objections were overruled and William Bacon was allowed to continue his damaging testimony.

When Court finally adjourned, Elena moved outside. Dorset and Hadley returned to the carriage to wait while Elena chatted with Jason. John Crown joined them and Elena introduced the two, then said, 'William Bacon hasn't spoken the truth.'

Dr Crown studied her. 'Aye. Keep calm though, Miss Blake. Tomorrow Lance will have the opportunity to relate his version.'

'But why would William Bacon do such a thing?'

Jason Jackson gazed at her soberly. 'Bacon knows that Lance will kill him when this is over. Lance challenged Bacon . . . if Bacon can see Lance hang, he'll escape a duel.'

Elena felt as if she had been transformed into a block of ice. 'They can't do that!' she cried.

Dr Crown grew solemn. 'Don't fret; perhaps things will change.'

Jason took Elena's hand. 'I need to get to the shop, Elena.'

'Thank you for coming,' she said. While he was striding away, Elena asked Dr Crown, 'How's Madeline?'

Crown's face relaxed into a smile. 'She's better.'

'Thank goodness.' She glanced at the Court-house door and saw the man with plaited hair emerge. She asked, 'Who is that man?'

He turned and frowned. 'That's Parnell Tanner. He and Lance are old enemies. I'm certain he hopes to see Lance hang.'

Elena glanced at the man again and met his gaze. He regarded her insolently and she turned her back. 'Why does he hate Lance?'

'He is a sea captain and a bloodthirsty pirate when he chooses. Once he captured one of Captain Merrick's ships. He slaughtered every man on board.'

'How dreadful!' she exclaimed.

John Crown's features darkened. 'Aye. Tanner had four vessels. Lance captured one, set it afire and sailed it to ram another of Tanner's ships. It cut Tanner's fleet in half and he has been following us since. He is after our Captain and his possessions.'

Dr Crown glanced again at Captain Parnell Tanner, then stated, 'That is why all four of Lance's ships ride at anchor in the harbour now. If we separate, Tanner will attack once we reach high seas.'

Without a glance William Bacon passed them and

climbed into a waiting carriage. Elena gazed after him. 'How can he lie?'

John shrugged. 'Easy when he may lose his own life if he doesn't.'

She looked up at Dr Crown. 'I hope they'll allow me to visit Lance.' She bade John Crown farewell and returned to the building which held Lance prisoner.

The guard gave her only ten minutes and the moment Lance entered the tiny room, she flung herself at him. 'Lance!'

He caught her in his arms and held her tightly.

'It's not fair what they're doing to you!'

'Aye,' he replied grimly, then he relaxed and smiled. 'Perhaps the trial's course will change tomorrow.'

She frowned angrily. 'If they do anything to you for rescuing that child, I shall put a ball through William Bacon's heart myself!'

Lance threw back his head and laughed. 'I do believe you would! Elena, only love could stir such passion as that!'

She blushed. 'Do not preen your feathers! They're laying it on like old Harry, and I can't bear to see you treated unjustly.'

'Elena, this is almost worth the trouble.'

'Lance Merrick, you're hopeless!' A thought occurred and she said, 'I talked with John Crown and he said Madeline is better.'

Lance's merriment disappeared. 'Yes, I saw John this morning early.' He whispered, 'She is aboard the *Sea Hawk*—my first mate has a child only a year younger than Madeline. When we sail, he'll take her to his wife in Pensacola.'

'Thank goodness,' she murmured. She frowned. 'Lance, Dr Crown told me about Captain Tanner.'

'He's Old Scratch in the flesh! That vulture would like to see a rope around my neck.'

A guard stepped inside and motioned to Elena. Too

embarrassed in someone else's presence to give Lance even a perfunctory kiss on the cheek, she started to leave. His arms tightened and he pulled her close.

'Lance, you mustn't! There's a guard . . .'

'If he had opportunity, he'd do the same,' he growled and leaned forward to kiss her quickly.

Her face flamed and she glared at him. 'You're wicked, Lance!'

He laughed and released her. Elena rushed from the room and could not bear to look at the guard.

She spent a restless, uneasy afternoon and night. The next morning she dressed in a striped gingham for the second day of the trial.

Accompanied by Dorset and Hadley, she once again slipped on to the back row to be seated. Within minutes after her arrival, Jason entered to join her.

Dr Crown and his fellow seamen appeared, behind them Captain Tanner. When William Bacon started down the aisle, he looked at Elena. Contemptuously, his gaze was direct before he walked to the front to be seated.

Looking at the back of William Bacon, Elena felt rage boil within. A side door opened and Lance entered. His blue eyes met hers and she smiled. She suspected John Crown must take Lance a change of clothes each day because he had on a fresh linen shirt and an immaculate white silk cravat. His dark green coat and doeskin breeches fitted flawlessly and his new Hessians gleamed.

Matthew Conway's impassive features gave no more clue to his feelings than did Lance's as the two moved towards the box.

Judge Lindsay was announced and everyone rose to their feet. To Elena's horror the web of lies had worsened as the trial continued. The clerk next summoned Roger Wyck.

A tall, stoop-shouldered man with gaunt cheeks and a

shaggy moustache shuffled forward and was sworn in. He gave his occupation as coachman for Horatio Kaufman. A jolt went through Elena when the man went on to testify that he had witnessed the fracas between Captain Merrick and Mr Kaufman.

In a nasal twang he stated that Kaufman had been set upon by the Captain, had drawn his pistol only to defend himself, then had been shot by Captain Merrick.

Instantly Matthew Conway was on his feet to shout, 'Objection!'

Fear and rage consumed Elena. Without pausing to give it thought, she leapt to her feet and cried, 'The man is lying! I was present and I saw it all!'

Pandemonium broke loose. Shouts erupted. One of Lance's men jumped up and in a flash crossed the room to punch William Bacon in the jaw.

Elena felt Jason Jackson's arm slip around her waist. Next, Dorset took her arm, but she could not hear what either of them were saying. She strained against Jason's hold, then looked at him and cried, 'Unhand me! I must tell them . . .'

'Miss Blake, it will do no good. They won't accept a woman's testimony. Here comes a deputy to remove you . . .'

Chaos rocked the courtroom. Fists flew, a chair crashed into a wall, while the gavel banged uselessly for order.

With Dorset and Hadley at their heels, Jason propelled Elena towards the door. She struggled to break free from Jason's grasp, but she could not. Before they reached the door, she glanced over her shoulder to look for Lance.

Momentarily he was hidden from view, then two men parted and she saw him standing with clenched fists, locks of dark hair in disarray over his temple. He looked at her, then past her at Jason and made a motion for Jason to get Elena out of the courtroom.

They hurried through the door and Lance was lost

from sight. Frustrated, Elena sobbed, 'Let me go! I beg you!'

Grimly, he kept his arm around her waist and rushed towards her carriage. Hadley ran ahead and within seconds they were inside. Jason jumped down from the carriage and slammed the door, Elena could hear his instructions to Hadley to make haste to his house, then they were on their way.

Sobbing, she threw herself into the corner. 'Dorset, the trial is filled with untruths! Why won't somebody listen?'

Finally they reached the Jacksons' and Mary met Elena at the door. While Mary led her inside and summoned a maid to fetch hot tea, Elena poured out the events of the trial.

Sinking down in a wing chair, Elena put her head in her hands. 'Mary, no one will listen. William Bacon will get Lance hanged to save himself from facing Lance over pistols.'

Mary's words of consolation were interrupted by the maid. As soon as the girl was gone, Mary closed the parlour door. She moved quietly to pour a steaming cup of tea. 'I should have been there with you.'

Elena raised her head. 'You couldn't have done anything. I didn't want to leave, but it was a good thing Jason saw to it that I did. My words will be no help to Lance.'

'It's not over yet,' Mary stated. 'Here, drink this.' She handed the cup to Elena, then poured another for herself. After a moment Mary said, 'Elena, I wanted to go, but Jason was determined that I stay home. Elena . . .' She paused and waited until Elena looked at her.

'Mary, what is it? You look overjoyed.'

'I shouldn't be when you're having so much trouble, but surely the truth will come out about Captain Merrick. Elena, I'm with child.'

For the first time in days Elena felt a surge of joy. She

exclaimed, 'I'm so happy for you!'

Mary smiled and blushed. 'Jason wants a girl and I want a boy!'

Elena listened to Mary's plans and for a time felt relief from the complications of the trial.

Jason had sent Hadley, the carriage and Dorset home when he deposited Elena at his house. As soon as he returned from the trial, Elena rose. It was a short distance to the court-house and she walked to visit Lance. She waited impatiently until the door opened and he was admitted. This time she did not hesitate to throw her arms around him. She gasped, 'What they're doing to you is dreadful!' She looked up at him.

A new bruise showed on his cheek, but otherwise he was the same. The corners of his mouth curled up in a grin. 'My little wildcat, if Jason hadn't forcibly removed you from the courtroom, you might be sharing this jail for contempt.' The smile faded and he regarded her solemnly.

'Elena, you must promise me that you won't attend the trial tomorrow.'

'Why not?'

'In the first place, I don't think Judge Lindsay will allow you into the courtroom. It's no place for you, Elena.' He relaxed and chuckled. 'You created quite a fuss today.'

'It's a nightmare and so unfair!'

He studied her intently. 'Can I believe that the worry in those green eyes is for me?'

She looked down and blushed. 'You were only going to Madeline Adams' aid. You shouldn't be prosecuted for defending yourself. That terrible William Bacon . . .'

His voice lost its lightness as he interrupted, 'Elena, promise me you won't attend.'

Reluctantly, she agreed. 'I'll wait, but you must tell Jason or John Crown to come at once and relate the outcome.' She suspected he was hiding the true reason he did not want her to attend—that he wanted to spare her hearing the verdict. Although he seemed as calm as ever, she guessed he feared the worst and it made her spirits sink.

He answered, 'John is coming to visit later today. I'll see to it that he'll relay everything to you.'

After a few more minutes the guard appeared to tell Elena it was time to leave. Lance kissed her farewell and she returned home.

The night was long, but the next day was worse. She paced the floor with agitation until she finally sighted John Crown coming through the gate. With one look at his solemn, angry countenance, she guessed his news.

She ushered him inside and faced him while he stated, 'He will hang in three days.'

For a moment she thought she would faint. He reached out to steady her. 'I'll be all right,' she murmured, 'I cannot believe they would do such a thing.'

The surgeon's face was grave. 'Aye. I shall see to William Bacon. Blast his lying hide!'

She placed her hand on John Crown's arm. 'Thank you for coming to tell me. I must go to Lance.'

'Yes.' He sighed. 'Farewell, Miss Blake.'

She closed the door behind him, then rushed upstairs to change her dress.

How could anyone face such a fate? She gazed at her dresses and wanted to look her prettiest for Lance. Finally she selected a green silk with emerald earrings and a tiny green bonnet.

The jailer smiled at her. 'Want to see Captain Merrick, Ma'am? He is having more than his share of visitors this afternoon. Reckon he's entitled to it, seeing as how he . . .' He looked at Elena and became silent. 'Sorry, Ma'am. This way.'

She waited in the familiar, hated room. When Lance entered, she flung herself into his arms while the tears sprang to her eyes.

'Elena! You do care!' He looked down at her and wiped away her tears with the ends of his cravat. He had shed the coat he usually wore in the courtroom, but was still clad in a soft white linen shirt with flowing sleeves, a snowy cravat, black breeches and boots. He regarded her and his voice deepened. 'But how much do you care?'

'I just don't want to see you hanged.'

He sighed. 'Elena, you do know how to dash a man's hopes, even when he faces death.'

'Oh, no!' she cried. 'I didn't intend any such thing. Lance, don't think about your fate.'

'Elena,' he stated, 'at least give me a farewell kiss before I hang.'

'Lance, please don't talk that way!'

'One kiss before my demise.'

'Oh, Lance!' she cried and threw her arms around his neck again, her lips against his. Her eyes fluttered wide and she caught him watching her. For one instant a vision came to her clearly. She could imagine the guard leading Lance to a scaffold. Her arms tightened around him and she started to kiss him passionately.

She pulled away a fraction and looked up. 'Lance, I can't bear for you to hang . . .'

Something flared in his eyes, such a flash of eagerness and hunger that for a moment she caught her breath and stopped talking. Her cheeks burned with embarrassment.

'Elena, my dearest,' he murmured huskily and his arms tightened around her. He leaned over her and gathered her against the length of his powerful body while his mouth touched hers tenderly.

With insistent relish he tasted the honeyed softness of her lips. His kiss became more ardent. Sensuously, his lips parted hers to coax her smouldering response into a throbbing blaze.

Breathless, she was shaken to the core of her being. He straightened to look down at her. Staring up at him, Elena stood dazed, befuddled with the depth of her emotion.

He started to speak, but just as he did so the guard entered to ask Elena to leave. Lance tilted her chin up and her heart beat with hammer-blows beneath his piercing study. She longed to wrap her arms around his neck and pull his mouth down to hers again to evoke the surging pleasures of the last few moments.

Lance brushed her cheek lightly with his lips, then Elena turned to hurry to her carriage.

Depression settled over her. It was impossible to accept the notion that Lance would hang. She wrung her hands and thought of what she could do. She would call on Governor Smythe and prevail upon him to listen. He must heed her story because Lance was innocent!

If only Lance had not challenged William Bacon in a fit of anger. She thought of Bacon's small, pale eyes and his wicked doings. She too, would like to put a ball through his heart. She clenched her fists and sat stiffly in the carriage. She reached home.

When she entered her bedroom, Dorset was behind the window, peering through a space between damask draperies and the window.

'Dorset, what in heaven's name?'

'My oath!' the maid exclaimed and jumped. She allowed the drape to fall shut, but glanced again at the window. 'A rum-start, Ma'am. I think somebody followed ye home.'

'Nonesense, Dorset! Don't be a giddy-goat! Come away from the window and summon Hadley. I intend to dispatch a request to the Governor for an audience.'

After Hadley had departed with the letter, Elena spent the rest of the afternoon and evening in gloom. Night was worse. It was impossible to sleep and she tossed restlessly, worrying over Lance's fate and remembering with unrelenting clarity his burning kisses.

Surely the Governor would not refuse to listen and once he heard her description of the circumstances surrounding Horatio Kaufman's demise, he would take action to halt the hanging.

The bright sunny morning lifted her spirits a degree. In an effort to cheer Lance, she dressed with care selecting a blue silk with tiny puff sleeves and rounded neck. It was scandalously low-necked for public view during the day, but she was certain Lance would be pleased. Trimmed with white ribbons, the bodice was secured with white silken bows over ruffles of white lace. Matching the dress, a small blue bonnet perched on top of her curls. She gathered parasol, mittens and reticule, then departed to visit the condemned.

His reaction was all she had hoped. Lance spun her around and gazed at her with obvious pleasure. 'How beautiful you look!' He drew her into his arms and held her against his broad chest.

Through his finely woven linen shirt, she felt once again the powerful muscles in his arms. His shirt smelled of smoke and straw. When he held her away, she noticed dark hair curling on his chest where shirt laces were loosened. Lance looked down at her.

Elena closed her eyes and lifted her mouth for his kiss. When none was forthcoming, she opened her eyes to gaze up at him.

He laughed. 'So, you do like my kisses!'

The rapscallion! Angrily she straightened, but his arms tightened and he laughed again. 'Ah, my wildcat! Takes little to stir your anger, I see.'

'Lance, you can be the most infuria . . .'

Her words ended, gone with thought as he pulled her close and kissed her. A wave of excitement washed over her. What she was allowing was not proper, but who would ever know? His fierce, unrelenting kiss provoked wanton pleasure and she felt safe in blissfully returning it.

She locked her arms around his neck and pressed against the length of his body. She caressed the back of his neck and wound her fingers in his luxurious black curls.

Discarding caution as a cumbersome burden, Elena's kisses explored with a relish matching his while her slender, pliant body arched beneath him.

He raised his head slightly to observe her. His voice was solemn and ragged. 'Elena, wed me now.'

She felt confused by his kisses; it was difficult to reason clearly and she uttered the first thing that came to mind.

'Whatever for, Lance? You would have nothing to gain by it.'

His sardonic amusement was sharp. 'Elena, someday you're going to learn that there is more to life than always getting a return for everything you do.'

The harshness left his countenance. 'Wed me now. Let me go to my grave knowing that you're my wife. Will you, Elena?'

She gazed up at him and considered his proposal. There was little to lose by consenting. He could make no demands she did not want to fulfill, it would last only two days, and—another thought occurred. Without hesitation, she uttered it aloud.

'If I do, then I'll be your widow and inherit your wealth.'

He drew a sharp breath and almost dropped her he released her so suddenly. 'You minx!' He gazed at her angrily.

His anger stirred Elena to her own. 'Nonsense! It's merely the truth. You know I'm not in love with you. Would you prefer for me to play-act and tease?'

He moved away, then gazed at her with stormy, hooded eyes. 'It might not be bad, Elena, for you to do so, since you'd have to exert the effort for only two days.'

'Cat's whiskers! You're angry and I didn't come to visit you to be scolded.' She retrieved her parasol.

Instantly he was beside her and his arms around her. His hands circled her waist while he looked down at her. 'Some day, Elena, I'll teach you a lesson.'

Chilled by the tone of his voice and the certainty of it, she reminded herself quickly that he could not carry out his threat.

He spoke quietly. 'You'll inherit my gold if you're my widow. Now will you wed me?'

She tilted her chin in the air. Half-aggravated, half-frightened of him, she would wreak her revenge on his cavalier manner. She answered in haughty tones, 'I am not certain now that I want to.'

His eyes flashed with anger, then he relaxed and smiled. His tone was cynical. 'You are giving up a great deal of gold, Elena. More than triple the worth of your inheritance.'

Startled, she looked up at him. More than triple her worth! Was he exaggerating, she wondered, then decided he was not. Why not consent—she had planned to wed him anyway. More than triple her own worth and it would all be hers . . .

She studied him; his blue eyes had a disturbing intensity. She spoke quietly.

'All right, Lance, I'll wed you.'

He tilted her chin upwards. 'What utter folly,' he whispered, then turned away. While he crossed to the door, she wondered why it would be folly. What had he meant? If she gained all his gold, it certainly would not be folly on her part. She studied his broad back speculatively.

He banged on the door and caused her to jump. In a second the door opened and Lance asked the guard to fetch the prison chaplain to perform a marriage ceremony. While the guard closed and locked the door, Lance looked around. He crossed to her and reached out to withdraw one of the pins from her hair. Carefully he twisted it into a ring.

'Hold out your finger so I can fashion this to fit,' he commanded gruffly. She did as he ordered.

From that moment until the quiet ceremony in the antechamber, Elena moved in a daze. Swiftness of events tinged the happenings with unreality. Finally she looked up into Lance Merrick's blue eyes and solemnly promised to take him as her lawful husband.

He kissed her briefly, then asked if she could return to his cell with him. The jailer promised half an hour only, then led them back to the narrow room.

Small and bare, it had one barred window in the oak door and another barred window in a wall. Above a scuffed and dusty floor, a bunk fashioned of raw pine was covered with straw. A washstand stood in the corner. Elena drew a sharp breath upon sight of his quarters.

The instant the key scraped in the lock, she faced him and stated, 'Lance, you said I would inherit your gold. Where is . . .'

He threw back his head and laughed, yet the sound had a bitter ring. His voice was filled with cynicism as he looked at her. 'When I dangle from a noose, Elena, will you see me up there or merely visions of gold?'

She frowned at him. 'Of course I don't want you to hang!' She started to mention the request she had sent the Governor to speak on Lance's behalf, but she bit back the words in fear Lance would laugh. 'You said you have a great deal of gold. I don't intend for some rascal to take what is mine.'

All amusement faded from his face and he gazed at her coldly.

When he remained silent, she asked, 'Are you going to reveal where it is?'

'No.'

She drew a sharp breath. 'You promised!'

He waved a hand at her impatiently. 'Three of my men

know. I'll make arrangements for one of them to reveal it to you.'

'Never!' she cried in consternation. 'They could easily cheat me of it. You're not keeping your part of the bargain.'

His eyes were glacial. 'I don't go back on my word, Elena.'

'You're impossible!' she snapped and headed for the door.

His hand closed on her arm and he turned her to face him. 'You vixen . . .' he murmured and swept her into his arms passionately.

Elena pushed against his chest without avail. His arms were inflexible. Suddenly she did not want the amorous attentions of her unpredictable new husband.

Then the certainty that she did not want his kisses began to diminish like a bank of snow under the noonday sun. Her struggles lessened. Her hands ceased pushing against his chest and lay still; her body no longer strained to pull away, but swayed towards his.

He shifted to kiss her cheek, then along her throat. Warm lips touched her shoulder and traced a line down the neck line of her low-cut gown to send tingles along her spine.

His fingers traced the smooth skin of her arms, catching her dainty hands and turning her palms for his lips to caress.

With deliberation he kissed each fingertip, then her palm and trailed his warm breath over her wrist to the crook of her arm.

Through half-closed eyes Elena gazed down at his dark hair. Her fingers slipped across the hard muscles in his shoulders.

A slow-burning fire rippled through her as Lance continued to kiss her shoulder, then the hollow of her neck. His breath was hot as he nuzzled her ear and whispered, 'I shall drive every thought out of that calculating mind of yours, Elena, except one.' His voice was husky. 'You are mine, Elena . . .'

She felt his hands at the ribbons of her dress, tugging the tiny bows free, unlacing the bodice to explore.

She moaned, 'Lance, stop.' The protest was a mere whisper. 'You mustn't.'

'You're my wife now, Elena. You have the smoothest skin on earth and a body ripe for love . . .'

Cool air hit her flesh and she stiffened. Lance peeled away the silken barrier, then his fingers deftly unfastened the chemise.

Twisting away, Elena tugged her dress up to cover her shoulders while she blushed hotly under his smouldering regard.

She gazed at him defiantly. 'You'll not undress me in a public cell!'

His features darkened and his words turned her to ice. 'I will if I damn please.'

She drew a sharp breath. 'Lance!' She glanced over her shoulder as if expecting to find the guard's leering face at the door. 'Please . . .'

For one instant she felt she had never faced such anger as she saw in his cold, blue eyes, then he deliberately turned his back.

His voice was bleak and harsh. 'Goodbye, Elena.'

She stared at his broad, implacable shoulders and suddenly wished they had not had such a stormy time. Reaching out to touch him, she started to say she was sorry, but the words died in her throat.

It took little to inflame his passions and he might do what she feared. She snatched up her belongings and made for the door to summon the guard.

The guard's grinning face did nothing to help and it was not until she was in the privacy of her carriage that she relaxed. Drained of emotion, she closed her eyes.

Mrs Edward Lancelot Pennington Merrick. Impossible to comprehend that she was wed. Why had he wanted to marry when it was useless?

At the sound of a carriage, she opened her eyes and leaned forward to look out of the window. A hackney halted and Dr Crown emerged, heading for the jail, obviously on his way to visit Lance.

She thought of Lance's ships and reputed wealth. She must find out about the gold. There was so little time left. By now, perhaps she would have a reply from the Governor.

Suppose Lance were set free! She felt hot at the thought, then forced contemplation of the possibility from her mind. It was too soon to consider.

A blast of wind shook the carriage and she heard the deep boom of thunder. Elena bit her lip with worry, then thoughts of Lance's kisses crowded out all reason. They turned along a square and she gazed at a small shop.

Impulsively, she called to the driver to halt. She would purchase a gift for Lance. It was ridiculous to acquire a present for a condemned man, but perhaps it would mollify his temper and he would realise it was a gesture of affection.

She halted, surprised at herself, then continued into the shop. So she did feel affection for him. Affection and something else . . . At remembrance of his caresses she trembled and it was an effort to contemplate her errand.

Recalling how his immaculate shirts had always caused him to appear so dark and handsome, she selected an elegant white cambric. When she returned to the carriage, yielding to an impulse, she asked the driver to halt at the Jacksons' house. Elena climbed down and hurried to tell Mary the news that she had just wed Lance.

To Elena's amazement, Mary already knew. While Jason stood on the portico, his wife ran out to throw her arms around Elena. Thunder rumbled in the distance and lightning streaked the sky. A gust of wind caused Elena to catch her bonnet. She held it tightly and asked Mary, 'How did you know?'

'Jason was home when Tom Trilling came by to tell him. You know anything that happens in Savannah is all over town within minutes!' Mary's eyes were filled with concern. 'It's so unfair and such a tragedy that Captain Merrick should be unjustly condemned.'

'Mary, he has been most foully accused and he was only trying to aid a child who needed someone's help desperately.'

Mary threw her arms around Elena again and both shed tears. Jason Jackson descended the steps to take them each by the arm and lead them inside for a cup of tea. While they drank the steaming liquid, wind rattled the panes as the storm approached.

Finally Elena rose and declared she must get home before the storm broke. Jason summoned Elena's driver, then the Jacksons followed her to the carriage and waited until Elena drove away.

Big drops of rain splashed against the carriage as it turned a corner. Elena held out her fingers and studied the crudely fashioned ring. Only a pin from her hair, yet strangely enough, it already held more significance than Alfred Crowe's large diamond ever had.

Her gloom deepened. She would have to keep occupied through the next nights and days to keep her thoughts off contemplation of Lance's fate. Suddenly a sob tore from her and she flung herself into a corner of the carriage to give vent to a storm of weeping. When the carriage halted and the door was held open for her, Elena managed to dry her eyes before going into the house.

Elena turned to hand her things to Hadley. His brown hair was hidden by a powdered wig, creases lined his brow, and his dark eyes regarded her gravely while Dorset hurried forward.

The maid snatched up a corner of her white apron to wipe away a tear. She gasped, 'Ma'am! 'Tis most dreadful! Thank the saints you are here. Pray you can undo this dreadful calamity!'

CHAPTER
SIX

IMPATIENCE shook Elena. 'Dorset, do stop this prattling! What are you talking about?'

Dorset gazed at Elena. 'Did you wed Captain Merrick, Ma'am?'

'Gracious sakes! Did they proclaim it from the jail roof?' Elena asked in exasperation.

'Saints preserve us!' Mumbling to herself, Dorset closed her eyes and began to pray.

'Dorset! In the name of heaven will you tell me what has transpired while I was gone!'

Dorset's eyes flew open. 'Men were here, Ma'am. They came from the Governor to take everything. They said you are wed to Captain Merrick who is a pirate. They've confiscated his ships . . .'

Elena reeled with shock. She reached out to grasp a table and steady herself. 'They've taken Lance's ships,' she whispered. 'They cannot!'

Startling her, a knock sounded at the door. Hadley moved to answer while Dorset wrung her hands.

''Tis them again!' Dorset muttered. 'I know 'tis them evil men.'

'Do hush, Dorset! Let me see if I can discover what is behind this,' Elena stated firmly. A wild fear enveloped her. Perhaps Lance was still a pirate. He had admitted to having been one before. Why had she consented to wed when she knew so little about her husband? Elena straightened and looked up as Hadley announced Mr Berkshire, the High Constable.

His dark hair was secured in a *queue* and he gazed at

her impassively. 'Mrs Merrick, may I have a word with you?'

Elena nodded and motioned, 'If you will come this way.' She entered the front parlour and closed the door as he strolled into the room. She turned to face him and locked her fingers behind her tightly.

'Mrs Merrick,' he began smugly and Elena hated his tone. 'Governor Smythe has learned that, in addition to being a murderer, the man you have just wed is also a pirate and has plotted to destroy Savannah!'

'That's impossible!' she gasped.

He gave her a condescending smile. 'How well do you know Captain Merrick, Ma'am? A seaman has sworn that Captain Merrick is carrying weapons for the Spanish in Florida to aid in an attack on Savannah.'

'He would never do such a thing!'

He said slyly, 'Captain Merrick is a handsome man, but how well do you know him? Have you ever been on board any of his ships?'

She shook her head. 'No, but . . .'

He interrupted, 'And have you known the Captain very long? A year . . .'

Anger shook her. 'No, only this April, as you must know, but that doesn't . . .'

Again he interrupted her, 'We have sworn testimony from men who know the Captain.'

'Who testified against Captain Merrick?' she asked.

'A man by the name of Points. Richard Points. He sailed on the *Dove*, one of the Captain's ships. Following a court order, a warrant was issued and all Captain Merrick's ships have been seized with the exception of the *Sea Hawk* which has eluded us.'

Relief flashed through Elena. Lance's flagship had escaped and at least Madeline Adams was safe.

The Constable continued gravely, 'According to law, a woman's property belongs to her husband, Mrs Merrick, therefore your possessions have been confiscated.'

'All my belongings! I can't lose them. They're mine, not Captain Merrick's!'

He shook his head. 'Not any longer. You're married to the man now and you know the law. Everything you own belongs to Captain Merrick, therefore is subject to confiscation. The man you wed is a renegade. Captain Tanner . . .'

'Who?' The name seemed to leap at her.

'Captain Tanner of the *Tiger's Tooth* was the first to come forth with information about Captain Merrick.'

Elena interrupted, 'The man is lying! He is lying just as William Bacon lied! Governor Smythe can't believe that!'

Constable Berkshire gazed at her sternly. 'I know, Mrs Merrick, it's shocking news when you've just wed the man, but there is no reason for Captain Tanner not to be truthful. Merrick is already condemned to hang. Captain Tanner will receive no gain from this act.'

'He's an enemy of Captain Merrick's. He's settling an old feud from their days at sea!' she protested.

Constable Berkshire stated sharply, 'I have my instructions, Mrs Merrick. As the wife of Captain Merrick, your possessions are now his, and his are subject to confiscation.' He looked around the room. 'You may keep your personal belongings and remain in this house.'

Elena trembled with rage. 'That's absurd! You know I'm his wife in name only!'

'That is your folly,' he replied. He gazed at her and spoke harshly. 'Your accounts have been seized.'

'You can't do such a thing! I'll have my marriage annulled!'

He shrugged. 'So be it, but until you do, it's the Captain's wealth and not yours.'

Fury enveloped her. 'This is an outrage! If I were a man, sir . . .'

'But you're not!' he snapped forcefully.

She shook and ordered, 'Get out of this house!'

He moved past her and closed the door. Snatching up a vase, Elena sent it crashing against the door behind him. With agitation she began to pace up and down when there was a knock.

Dorset opened the door cautiously. Tears streaked her face and she entered the room. 'Ma'am, 'tis dreadful . . .'

'Dorset, please fetch my cape and ask Hadley to summon Perkins. I need a carriage because I intend to call on Matthew Conway, my husband's attorney.'

Over an hour later in the steady, cold rain which followed the storm, Elena returned to her carriage from Matthew's house. In a corner Dorset huddled and twisted a handkerchief between her fingers. 'Can he help you, Ma'am?'

Elena sank down on the seat. 'It'll be a lengthy process. What can I do? Why did I ever consent to wed?'

'It was a kindness to a condemned man,' Dorset whispered. 'Ma'am, begging your pardon, but we should return home. We might catch the ague,' she paused and her voice dropped, 'and I'm certain we are watched.'

'Dorset, do not tell me that one more time!' Elena snapped impatiently. 'There are no footpads in Savannah!' She became silent while her mind raced over the dilemma. Lance was worth a great deal, but suppose his gold was on board his ships! It could either be confiscated or on the *Sea Hawk* sailing away from Georgia. 'Confound Lance Merrick!' she whispered, then realised it could also be in a bank somewhere. Her eyes narrowed. She raised her voice to order the coachman to the jail.

'Saints preserve! Ye cannot go to such a place at this hour. They will not allow ye inside.'

'Yes, they will!' Elena snapped and Dorset became silent.

Within minutes the carriage slowed and halted. Elena

entered and swept up to the desk. The startled guard looked up, then rose to his feet. 'Evening, Ma'am.'

'I must see my husband, Captain Merrick!'

The man's eyes widened and he reached for a key. 'Aye, Ma'am, this way.'

Elena followed the man as he led the way back to Lance's tiny cell. A lantern swung from a hook and cast a warm light over Lance's features. He frowned as he rose to meet her.

'Elena, something's happened . . .'

All the way from Matthew Conway's house, she had mentally rehearsed how she would lead up to revealing the dilemma to Lance, but her planned speech fled. She could not bear to mince words and interrupted him.

'They've confiscated your ships!'

'What?'

'They think you're a pirate plotting against Georgia. The Governor has issued a warrant to confiscate all your property. Because I'm your wife, they've taken everything I own!'

His hands closed over her shoulders painfully. 'Where are my ships?'

She drew a sharp breath and grasped his arms. 'I've lost everything!'

He shook her slightly. 'Answer me, damnit! Where are my ships?'

'I told you, they've been confiscated. You rogue! Out of sentiment I agreed to wed; now, I've lost everything because of you.'

He blanched and his fingers bit painfully into her flesh while he swore. 'All four ships gone . . .'

'No, the *Sea Hawk* escaped. They have the other three.' She gazed at him and added, 'You've wrecked my life! Now you must tell me where to find your gold!'

His jaw clamped shut and he turned away to stare at the wall. She grasped his arm. 'How can you do this?'

He pounded his fist against his palm. His voice was

harsh as he asked, 'How could they? There is no legality to it.'

She spoke quickly. 'The judge has issued a warrant for seizure because witnesses have testified that you're a pirate and a traitor carrying weapons to the Spanish in Florida to help attack Savannah.'

'Impossible!' His eyes narrowed. 'Who testified?'

She replied, 'Captain Tanner.'

Lance swore, then laughed bitterly. 'So, Elena, you're not the only one conniving to gain my fortune.' He tilted his head. 'You said "witnesses"—who else?'

She thought a moment. 'Constable Berkshire said a seaman from your *Dove* by the name of Richard Points.'

Lance was silent a moment, then expelled his breath. 'Aye. He was booted off in disgrace for stealing from his shipmates.' He looked at her and said softly, 'So the *Sea Hawk* escaped.'

'Yes,' she answered. 'Madeline will be safely away.'

His eyebrow arched. 'Oh ho! You do have a thought for someone else.'

'Lance, where is your gold?'

He gazed at her in silence. He had threatened to teach her a lesson for her continual concern over his fortune and she pondered if that was his object at the moment. She asked, 'Will you tell me?'

'No.'

'I hope they hang you tomorrow!' she snapped.

He drawled, 'What were those remarks a moment ago about marrying me out of sentiment?' His eyes narrowed and he grasped her shoulders agin. 'My conniving little saucebox! All you know is gold. You were raised that way and they did a thorough job. I'll not reveal where my gold is, Elena.'

She shook with fury. 'Damn you, Lance Merrick!'

He grinned suddenly. 'My, my! What words from such a dainty lady.'

She was overwhelmed with rage and frustration. His

teasing grin was more than she could cope with. Tears sprang to her eyes and she reached out to beat against his chest. 'I hate you! You promised me and now you're breaking it. Because of you I have nothing . . .'

He pulled her against him and she sobbed. His arms were tight and warm; she felt his hand stroking her hair until she quietened. She looked up at him to whisper, 'Why are you so cruel one moment and so kind the next?'

His countenance was sober and he glanced over her head towards the door, then picked her up and moved to sit on the bunk in the far corner of the cell.

'Elena,' he whispered, 'keep your voice down.'

Now what was he up to, she wondered. She merely nodded.

He brushed a tendril of hair away from her face. 'I haven't revealed the location of my gold because I didn't think it would be necessary.'

'Why?' she stared at him with a puzzled frown.

'I intend to escape from here.'

'Esca . . .'

He placed his fingers against her lips. 'Shh. John Crown has planned it. Since the ships have been confiscated, it may be more difficult . . .' His blue eyes were worried. 'It may be impossible. I didn't want to reveal anything to you because I didn't think it would be necessary, but now . . . I might not get out.'

She studied him solemnly. 'Even if you escape—why wouldn't you trust me to know?' A twinge of anger touched her. 'Were you afraid I would take your gold?'

'Parnell Tanner wants it. He knows we're wed. Elena, it could be dangerous for you to know.'

'Was that the true reason?' she said, 'I'm not afraid of that Captain Tanner. When do you think you'll escape?'

'Tomorrow if all goes well.'

'Can I help?'

He shook his head. 'No. I think the less you know

about it, Elena, the better off you'll be. In case I don't, I'll relate the whereabouts of my fortune.'

She nodded and he looked around. 'I need quill and paper to draw a map. Just a moment.' He rose and placed her on the bunk, then crossed to the door to pound on it. When the guard appeared Lance said he wanted to write a will and needed quill and paper. As soon as the guard had furnished the items and closed the door again, Lance moved to the bunk.

He leaned down to pick her up and Elena protested, 'Lance! It's not proper.'

He laughed and ignored her protests to lift her on to his lap. 'We're wed, Elena, we're alone and I'm sentenced to hang soon. I give not a damn for silly proprieties.' Keeping an arm around her waist, he handed her a small bottle. 'Please hold the ink.'

She did so and listened while he talked. 'I've sailed all over the world and put in at ports in this new land. Have you heard of a river called Mississippi?'

She shook her head. 'No.'

'It's far in the interior. Cutting across this land, through wilderness, it opens into the sea. At its mouth is New Orleans; above New Orleans is another town— Natchez.'

'Is this far from Savannah, Lance?'

He sighed. 'By ship 'tis merely some two thousand miles from Savannah.' He shifted the paper. 'Look here, Elena.'

The quill scratched against the paper while he depicted the Atlantic coastline of America. He sketched in boundary lines for Georgia and, south of it, Florida. Far to the west of Savannah was the Mississippi River. At its mouth Lance made a cross representing New Orleans, and close above it, another cross for the town of Natchez. He looked up at her.

'Now, Elena, there are only two ways to get to New Orleans and Natchez. One is by land.'

She looked at him while he bent over the paper and sketched. Dark locks of hair curled over his temples and a rough stubble of whiskers darkened his chin. The white linen shirt was damp from her tears. She gazed at his blunt, strong fingers holding the map. He spoke softly.

'You can travel north through the Cumberland Gap, then float down the Mississippi, but that would be a tremendous journey filled with hardships and would take a long time.' His finger traced a direct line from Savannah to New Orleans and he continued, 'To get from Georgia to Louisiana Territory directly would mean forging your way across a wilderness that in many areas has never been explored. It would cover land that is rugged, mountainous, inhabited by Indians and wild animals.'

He raised his head and gazed at her. 'The other way to get from Savannah, Georgia, to New Orleans is by sea.' His quill traced a line from Savannah's port southward while he explained, 'From here sail south down the coast of Florida and around its tip, then head north into the Gulf. Heading north and west across the Gulf, a ship can easily reach the mouth of the Mississippi River.' He looked at her. 'That's the way to get to New Orleans, Elena.'

A suspicion was growing and she gazed at him with consternation. 'Lance, do you have any gold in Savannah?'

He laughed and shook his head. 'Not a sovereign.'

She stiffened and looked down at the map. 'Is it in New Orleans?'

He shook his head again. 'No, but to get to it you'll have to travel to New Orleans, then north to Natchez.'

'That's impossible!' She gazed in horror at the map. 'It might as well be in China!'

His blue eyes were steadfast as he looked at her. 'You wanted to know this.'

She sighed. 'Very well. Is it in a bank in Natchez?'

Impatience shook her as he answered in the negative. She clamped her lips together and glared at him while he continued, 'It's north of Natchez, Elena. In 1795, the American Envoy, Thomas Pinckney, signed a treaty with Spain guaranteeing Americans' right to navigate the Mississippi River. Now people in the interior send their goods down river by barge or flatboat to New Orleans. River currents are too strong to return home in such a manner, so everyone travels homeward over land. There's an old buffalo trail which later was used by Indians; this trail is the means for travellers to journey inland to their homes. This trail is called the Natchez Trace. From Natchez it winds north for five hundred miles to Nashville, Tennessee.'

While he talked he reached up to unfasten her cloak, then he gently untied the ribbons to her bonnet. Elena paid little heed to his actions; her thoughts were on the map. She placed her finger on the paper. 'You mean I should take a ship from here, sail around Florida to New Orleans, then travel north to Natchez. At Natchez I take this Trace . . .' she paused and looked up at him. 'Where do I go from Natchez?'

His fingers closed around her hand and his blue eyes darkened. 'You don't go anywhere. Elena, I'm revealing the location of a fortune, but it would be impossible for you. If something happens to me, you must get John Crown or Jason to see to this. If John returns to Savannah he would be the one. He was with me before and he knows exactly where the gold is buried.' Deftly, he shoved her cloak off her shoulders. He contained, 'If you must go to Jason, give him the map. He can hire trustworthy men to fetch the treasure for you.'

'Lance, exactly where is this fortune? What town is it in?'

A corner of his mouth lifted in a crooked grin. 'There is no town, Elena. It's a few miles off the Natchez Trace buried in the wilderness beneath cypress trees.'

Rage shook her. 'Lance Merrick, how can I get it out of a wilderness! It might as well be at the bottom of the sea!'

She started to jump to her feet, but his arm tightened and held her on his lap. 'Shh!' he admonished quickly. 'Keep your voice down! Elena, Parnell Tanner would like nothing better than for you to go after my gold.'

'What has that to do with the matter?' she asked.

'I'm certain this double-dealing by Parnell is not only out of revenge, but also to try to find my gold. When he attended my trial, he was searching for this opportunity.'

'What opportunity, Lance?'

'If I hang, he knows someone will go after the treasure.' He regarded her soberly and traced his finger along her cheek. 'That's why I didn't want to reveal this to you. You must take this map and hide it carefully, Elena. Wait and see if I escape. If not, then get the map to Jason or John and let them handle the matter. If Tanner remains in town, don't give any indication that you have a map or have ever seen one. He would get the information from you within minutes.'

He turned her face up to gaze at her. 'Elena, tell Jason about Parnell Tanner. Jason mustn't underestimate how dangerous the man is.' A corner of Lance's mouth raised and he grinned ruefully. 'A sin which I've committed and am suffering consequences for this moment.'

'The villainous wretch!' she murmured.

He looked at her. 'Elena, you're no match for the likes of Tanner. If he learns I've revealed this to you, he'll take the treasure and you along with it. He's cruel beyond belief—a more devilish fiend has seldom walked this earth.'

His blue eyes grew cold. 'I should like to face Tanner in a fight. We have an old score to even.'

Elena turned his hand over and ran her finger lightly across the calloused palm. She looked up at him and whispered. 'You should never have had to leave England.'

His gaze shifted to her and he shrugged one shoulder. 'There's no looking back, Elena. I have no family there who wants me. I needed to change.'

'How so?'

'I accepted too many things in life without question. I've learned more about my own capabilities.' He became solemn. 'Elena, warn Jason about the Natchez Trace—that it's a path through a rugged wilderness, filled with dangers—wild animals, swamps, and brigands. People call it "The Devil's Backbone". Many a man has started home from New Orleans to disappear along the Trace.'

'Lance, where is the gold?'

He sighed. 'Look here.' He began to draw. The quill tickled her knees as he scratched lines on the paper. 'Tell Jason to head out of Natchez along the Trace.' He began to make tiny drawings on the map—a tavern, a creek crossing the Trace, burned trees, a large stump.

Elena shifted slightly and his arm tightened around her waist. His voice was low as he said, 'Now, here is where you leave the Trace—there is a tall oak which is split in two, most likely by lightning. It's a good landmark. Turn east at that tree.'

He drew several tiny lines in a row and she asked, 'What's that?'

'A swamp—low land covered with water. Some places it's ankle-deep, other places it comes to the knees, but it's shallow.'

Swiftly, he sketched the path, then started to explain his drawing. While she concentrated on his words, his fingers trailed across her temple, down her cheek and throat, behind her neck. His thumb moved back and forth against the nape of her neck. Finally he gazed at her and asked, 'Do you understand my instructions?'

She gazed at the sketch. 'Yes,' she murmured.

'Do you think you can explain this clearly to Jason if he is the one to get it?'

She nodded and looked at him. 'Lance, how much gold is there?'

He leaned forward and kissed her neck lightly. His breath smelled faintly of tobacco as he murmured in her ear, 'I have five trunks, Elena. Two are buried near the first cypress—there.' His hand rested on her knee while he pointed to the drawing.

'About one hundred yards farther east are three buried beneath another cypress. One trunk holds coins, three hold ingots, while the last is filled with precious stones.' His voice became cynical. 'More than you've ever owned.'

She drew a breath sharply and felt a flare of relief. 'How many know this, Lance?'

'I do and three of my men—Jeremy Billingslea, John Crown and Maynard Plunkett.' He turned her face to gaze into her eyes. 'Elena, warn Jason of all the dangers involved. This is a perilous place and Tanner wants my fortune.'

His arms tightened around her and he kissed her lightly. He paused, then kissed her again; this time for longer. He raised his head slightly. 'Fold the map, Elena, and guard it carefully. Get it to Jason as soon as possible.'

He placed the quill on the floor and took the bottle of ink from her hands to do the same. Elena folded the stiff paper into a small square and dropped it into her reticule.

While she drew the strings tightly together and slipped them over her wrist, Lance kissed the back of her neck, then pulled her into his arms.

Dimly she was aware of his hands against her head until long, silky strands of hair streamed over his arm in a shimmer of gold.

With her face raised to his, he kissed her languorously, arousing her as she lay in his arms.

Tugging free the bows of her bodice, his calloused fingers pushed away blue silk and stroked her satiny flesh.

Like a captain taking charge of his ship, his hot-blooded passion guided her response. Gasping with pleasure, Elena felt on fire from each caress, each touch of his lips on her eager body.

Never in her life had she experienced what he was stirring now. She lost all apprehension of interruption by a guard. Vanished was the stark, squalid cell. Nothing on earth existed except this man, his broad shoulders, the length of his powerful body, his deft hands. She was lost like a novice mariner in a windswept tempest.

Lance's thick curls wound smoothly around her fingers while a stubble of whiskers scraped her skin.

Charting his way with feathery touches and passionate kisses, Lance provoked a surging desire. As her shy hesitancy burned away in molten longing, his hard male body became a wonder to explore.

Elena's pliant abandonment underwent transformation. Enraptured, she returned caresses, matched male ardour with unrestrained delight. She thrilled to stroke his furred chest, to feel the ripple of tough sinewy muscles beneath her fingers.

Groaning, he shifted and held her away.

She tugged against his neck to draw him down again. 'Lance,' she whispered, 'please . . . come here.' Her long-lashed eyelids fluttered open and she gazed at him.

His face was as dark as a thundercloud. 'No.' A muscle worked in his jaw as he elaborated, 'Not here, Elena. I'll not have you remember for the rest of your life that you were taken for the first time in a miserable, dirty cell.'

'Lance,' she purred and twisted against him. She cared not about his argument nor did the surroundings signify. She wanted the lean, powerful body close; she longed for his mouth upon hers.

He rose and stood her unceremoniously on her feet.

Startled, she frowned. While she looked at him reality filled her.

He was gazing at her with unabashed admiration. She looked down and discovered her open bodice revealed pink-tipped ivory flesh. Instantly she began to draw her laces. 'You're the most aggravating creature on earth!' she snapped. Sanity and embarrassment came in like an ocean wave. 'How can I let you cause me to lose all reason?' she grumbled.

He lifted her chin and spoke with a mocking lightness. 'You can't stop me because of your own hot blood, Elena.'

'I'll come tomorrow, Lance.'

His perusal was insolent as he lowered his gaze in a deliberate appraisal. 'You were meant for a man, Elena. That's as certain as sunrise.'

His words inflamed banked fires. She breathed softly, 'Oh, Lance . . .'

'Go quickly, Elena,' he whispered in a hoarse voice, 'before I forget all my good intentions.'

She banged on the door. The moment the jail door closed behind her, she dashed for the carriage. Raindrops were cold against her cheeks; she glanced ahead and saw the horse standing patiently. Lightning flashed in a jagged streak. In its quick, cold light a movement caught her eye. Elena gasped as she saw a rider move into the shadow of a building.

Suddenly she was acutely conscious of the map. She clutched her reticule against her side and climbed into the carriage. Her heart thudded violently. There had been no mistaking the width of the man's shoulders she had just glimpsed—or the braided hair beneath his floppy hat.

She settled in the carriage and faced Dorset. The

maid's face looked pinched with worry and fright. As the vehicle commenced to move, Dorset whispered, 'I know we're watched, Ma'am!'

'You are right,' Elena whispered.

'Great saints! You saw him too! That devil what was at court. Miss Elena, we mustn't travel abroad at this hour.'

While Dorset talked, Elena pondered the situation. She slipped her hand into the reticule and withdrew the map. Should she halt at the Jacksons' and give it to Jason now? She thought of their expected baby and realised she dared not involve Jason with Parnell Tanner. Also, the *Sea Hawk* might be on the high seas never to return to Savannah. How could she ask either John Crown or Jason to get the buried trunks?

Even more worrisome was the thought that Parnell Tanner might suspect she had a map or knew the location of Lance's fortune. Shivering, she clutched the reticule tighter.

Louisiana Territory—she had heard Uncle Findley speak of it, but had given little attention to what he had said. She had never heard of Natchez or the Trace. '*The Devil's Backbone*,' Lance had called it. Her hands were cold and her trembling worsened. How had her life become so complicated in such a short time? It was all Lance Merrick's fault. She should never have met him that morning . . . yet, she did not regret doing so. For a moment she thought of his passionate kisses and forgot the terrors of the night.

Dorset whispered, 'Could the Captain help ye?'

'Perhaps, Dorset.' She debated whether to reveal everything to the maid. Never had Elena hesitated to tell Dorset anything, but this time she was fearful it might place Dorset in danger from Tanner.

Twisting in the seat, Elena moved the leather flap to gaze out of the window. The street appeared deserted. The horse made a steady clop against cobblestones.

Lightning revealed bright colours of blooming flowers and darkened houses.

When she reached home, Elena stepped to the window and shifted the curtain to look out again. Behind her Dorset whispered, 'Do you see anything, Ma'am?'

Elena studied the street and yard; there was no sign of horse or rider, but she could not shake the feeling that Parnell Tanner was out there. A cold fear gripped her as she turned from the window.

Dorset hovered behind her and whispered, 'Is there anyone near, Ma'am?'

Elena shook her head. 'I don't see anyone, Dorset.' The maid turned for the stairs and Elena headed for the door to speak to Hadley. She clutched her reticule tightly in her hand, conscious of the map tucked inside. Hadley was locking up for the night when she spoke to him.

'Would you ask Perkins to remain in the back room tonight?'

If it seemed a strange request, the footman gave no indication, but merely nodded and replied, 'Aye, Ma'am.'

She hesitated, then inquired, 'Hadley, do you know how to use a pistol?'

He smiled. 'Aye, Ma'am.'

'Would you keep it handy? Tonight, Dorset and I thought someone was following us home.'

His smile disappeared and he gazed at her solemnly. 'Would you like me to remain by the door?'

'No. Thank you, but that shouldn't be necessary. If you'll speak to Perkins, that should be sufficient.'

When he nodded, she sighed with relief. She mounted the stairs and headed for her room. When she was dressed in a warm gown, Elena extinguished the lamps and peeped out of the window.

A gust of wind blew a spray of raindrops against the pane, then lightning flashed. Below, everything appeared normal. The coach house was dark and Elena hoped Perkins was in the servants' room downstairs. Remembrance of the brief, momentary glimpse of Parnell Tanner at the court-house came to mind. Elena shivered and moved to the chiffonier and picked up the map. She gazed at it a moment, then looked around the room.

It should be hidden, she decided, but where would be a good spot? Eliminating first one place, then another, she walked around. Finally she opened the armoire, removed a slipper and pushed the map down into the toe. After she closed the armoire, she crossed the room to climb into the high feather bed.

Once settled, she gazed at the windows and watched raindrops form rivulets and run down the panes. Sleep was impossible. She felt tense and wary. Every blast of wind that shook the house, each creak of timbers increased her worry.

Across the back of a chair lay the blue dress she had worn. *My wedding dress*, she thought. *Mrs Merrick*. It seemed impossible and unreal.

Lance was planning an escape. She wished now that she had asked more questions. Would he come to her house? What was she to do? Suppose John Crown did not return to Savannah? She could not bear to consider that Lance might hang and tried to stop thinking about the *Sea Hawk* and Dr Crown.

She dozed fitfully. During the night Elena awakened. Quietly, she lay staring into the gloom. She heard a scrape. A shiver ran up her spine because the noise had not been timbers creaking in the wind.

Downstairs something thumped. Elena stiffened and gazed intently at the door. All was quiet. Had it been Perkins or Hadley moving around?'

She threw back the covers and rose. Pulling on a robe she moved to the door and opened it a crack.

While her feet grew cold, she listened. Just as she was

about to close the door, she heard a tinkle. Her ears strained at the eerie noise. Trying to think of all possibilities to explain such a sound, Elena peeked into the hall. There was no one to be seen.

It could be Hadley or Perkins or even Dorset she reminded herself. Elena thought of the two armed men asleep in the house. Resolutely, she picked up a taper to light a candle.

There should not be any danger with Hadley and Perkins at hand, she reasoned. She was determined to discover the source of the frightening noises.

Pulling her robe tightly beneath her chin, Elena stepped into the hall. She whispered, 'Hadley?'

There was no answer. Flickering candlelight threw elongated shadows on the wall. Elena crossed to the stairs and slowly descended. Prickles ran along her spine and she chided herself for being foolish. Everything appeared as usual except the library door was closed.

Trying to remember if it had been open earlier, Elena stood in the centre of the front hall and gazed around. Chilled to the bone, she glanced upstairs. Hadley slept in an attic room which seemed far away now that she was downstairs. She gazed in the direction of the room where Perkins should be sleeping.

A snap made Elena jump. Her heart pounded with fright as she looked hard at the closed library door. She felt certain someone was moving about in that room.

Her hand shook and the tiny flame danced crazily sending grotesque shadows around her.

Suddenly the flame blew out and she was plunged into darkness.

CHAPTER
SEVEN

ELENA opened her mouth to cry for Perkins when a heavy hand clamped over her face and cut off her call. Roughly, an arm circled her waist and she was picked up, then carried through the darkness.

In vain she struggled. The library door opened and they moved inside. Foul breath struck her as her captor breathed heavily while he growled, 'Not a peep out of you! You scream when I remove my hand and I'll slit your throat!'

He released her and she turned to face Parnell Tanner. For an instant faintness washed over her. He was a giant; the angry scowl on his face and the long, thin dagger in his hand made him even more terrifying.

Elena swayed, then steadied herself by gripping the back of a chair.

He seemed to notice and chuckled. 'That's better. Now, where is Merrick's treasure?'

'I don't know what you're talking about,' she whispered.

Instantly the knife was at her throat. Its sharp point felt like a needle against her skin. Elena could not breathe; she stiffened and stepped back.

He followed and reached out to wind his fingers in her hair. 'Where's the treasure? Don't lie to me!'

'It's on board the *Sea Hawk*,' she answered.

'Wench!' His hand wound cruelly in her hair and she gasped. 'I know it's not. Nor is it in Savannah.'

'Let me go!' Elena cried and bit her lip.

'Where is it?'

'I don't know.'

He pulled harder and tears sprang to her eyes. His free hand gripped her arm painfully. Finally Elena could stand no more. 'It's thousands of miles away!' she cried.

He hauled her close. 'Tell me exactly where or I'll carve my initials on you. Don't lie because I already know some facts about it.'

His grip on her hair did not loosen and he continued to hold her arm tightly. Elena gasped. 'It's near . . .' For an instant she thought wildly. How much did he know? She said, 'It's near New Orleans—to the west of town.'

His eyes narrowed causing her heart to thud violently. He asked, 'How far west?'

'Fifteen miles,' Elena fabricated her story. If only there were some way to summon help.

'Then there has to be a map. Where is it?' He tightened his hold.

'Oh, please stop!'

For the first time he relaxed his terrible tug on her hair. 'Where's the map?'

She straightened and faced him. There had to be some way to escape—if only for a moment to alert Perkins. She looked around the room, then answered, 'It's in this room.'

His eyes narrowed. 'Where?'

She bit her lip in indecision. He raised his hand and she spoke quickly, 'It's hidden in the fireplace.'

His hands dropped away. 'Get it,' he ordered.

While she mulled over various courses of action, Elena turned towards the hearth. If she screamed it would take too long before Perkins or Hadley would reach the library. In that time Tanner could use his wicked dagger on her.

She looked at the tools for the fire. A poker lay on the hearth. Suddenly Elena screamed for help and snatched up the poker.

Instantly Tanner leapt towards her. She saw the flash of the dagger's blade. Gritting her teeth, Elena swung the poker with all her might.

It struck his wrist and sent the dagger flying through the air.

With terrifying ease he snatched the poker from her hands and flung it across the room. Elena turned to run.

There was a commotion in the hall. Voices sounded and Hadley called out.

Elena screamed again, then glanced over her shoulder. Tanner was swinging his legs over the windowsill. While she watched, he dropped out of sight.

The door burst open and Hadley appeared with a pistol. Elena pointed towards the open window and gasped, 'He's out there!'

A babble of voices could be heard, then Perkins came in and behind him came Dorset. Elena told Perkins where Hadley had gone and the coachman headed for the window.

Reaction set in and Elena sank down in a chair. Violent trembling shook her and, burying her head in her lap, she started to cry. Dorset rushed to her side.

'Miss Elena! What happened? Have you been harmed?'

Elena raised her head and wiped away tears. 'No, Dorset. That man was so dreadful . . .'

'I'll get you a tot of brandy. It'll soothe your nerves.' She turned and hurried away.

Elena heard a shout outside and shivered. She massaged her scalp and thought about Tanner. Lance had to escape! If he did not, her own life would be worth nothing. She rose to her feet unsteadily and went over to the window.

Hadley and Perkins were searching the yard. The rain had changed to a fine mist and Elena knew both men were getting soaked uselessly. She called to them to come inside and headed for the front door to unlock it.

She faced both servants and explained that Tanner thought she had something he wanted. She described him fully and asked them to be watchful.

When she headed for her room, she met Dorset in the upstairs hall. 'Ma'am, I put brandy on a table by your bed. Would you like me to stay awhile?'

She patted Dorset's hand. 'No, thank you, Dorset. I'll be all right.'

Sleep seemed impossible. Thoroughly chilled, Elena could not bear the thought of retiring to bed. Would Tanner come back? The question was too dreadful to be faced. He might well try again. Elena shivered and sipped the small glass of brandy.

She felt the warmth as it went down. A knock at the door startled her. Dorset's voice sounded.

'Come in, Dorset.'

The maid thrust her head into the room. 'Miss Elena, let me come stay with you like I used to do when you were a child. I'll lay on the chaise.'

She sighed. 'Very well, Dorset.' It was a relief to have her in the room. Elena removed her robe and climbed into bed while Dorset blew out the last candle.

For a time Elena lay stiffly staring into darkness, but finally she relaxed and sleep came.

The next thing she was aware of was Dorset calling her name.

'Ma'am, you are wanted downstairs. The High Constable is here again.'

Groggy and befuddled, she struggled to wake. As she climbed out of bed, she noticed the candles and darkened windows. 'What time is it, Dorset?'

'Four o'clock. Ma'am, Captain Merrick has escaped!'

Exultation filled her. 'Escaped! That's why the Constable is here. I can't see him like this. Tell him I'll be down shortly,' she ordered, and began to dress hurriedly.

She felt like singing for joy. Lance was free! He would

not hang! Soon he would come to get her and she would be safe from Tanner. She smiled into the mirror and hummed a tune as she tied her hair behind her head. She smoothed the ruffles on the sleeves of her calico dress and thought of deep blue eyes and Lance's wicked smile.

When she saw the men milling about in the hall below, her smile disappeared. To her consternation, she discovered Constable Berkshire had a warrant and wanted to search the house for Lance. Elena waited stonily while a perfunctory search commenced; a young deputy was instructed to wait with her.

Several times the deputy glanced at Elena. Finally he spoke. 'Ma'am, don't worry.' He whispered, 'Your husband is safely away.'

Elena regarded him. 'What are you talking about?'

He glanced upstairs in the direction of the Constable, then whispered, 'They know he's gone. Constable Berkshire is merely doing his duty. Your husband is out of their reach.'

Elena gazed into wide brown eyes. 'Where is Captain Merrick?'

'He escaped on one of his ships, the *Sea Hawk*. One of the Governor's ships followed it out of the harbour. Constable Berkshire knows he's gone, but they want to cover all possibilities.'

Elena's joy and hope dwindled to nothing at the young man's words. Cold fear set in. If the *Sea Hawk* had sailed . . . when would Lance return? Or would he ever return? Even if he wanted to, could he get past Constable Berkshire and his deputies?

Worriedly, she bit her lip, then realised the deputy was speaking to her.

'Are you all right, Ma'am?'

She nodded. 'I'm fine.' She turned away and informed Hadley, 'I'll be in the front parlour if the Constable wants me.'

Elena moved across the hall and into the darkened

room. Even with the house full of people, she could not
bear the dark. Memory of Tanner was too clear. She lit
one of the lamps and wrung her fingers together. What
could she do? Lance had sailed . . . it could be months
and months before he would return.

There was no one to protect her from Parnell Tanner.
Hadley and Perkins could just do so much and no more.
As long as she remained in Savannah, she would be in
jeopardy unless the man had followed Lance. She rejected that possibility. He would find it easier to wring
the information from her than deal with Lance. Also,
she realised that if Tanner stayed behind, he would need
to get the information from her quickly or he would not
have a chance to get the treasure.

Lance could have sailed to get it, then return to
Savannah. She ran her fingers across her temple. What
could she do to protect herself? No matter how cautious
she was, there would be no way to stop Captain Tanner
from accosting her again—unless she was not available
for him to do so.

Gazing into space, she mulled over the possibility. In
the doorway Hadley cleared his throat and announced
the Constable.

Elena followed Constable Berkshire to the front door
while he informed her that he was leaving men to guard
both front and back doors in case Lance should appear.

When Hadley closed the door behind the officer,
Elena returned to the parlour to consider what action to
take. In her judgment there were only two courses open
to Lance. He might return to Savannah, which was
highly risky, if not impossible now. If he did not return,
she felt certain he had sailed for Natchez to get the
treasure.

She pondered what she should do; finally she made a
decision and summoned both Hadley and Dorset. As
soon as they entered the parlour, Elena closed the door
and faced her two most trusted servants.

She explained about her husband's treasure and Parnell Tanner. She took a deep breath and continued, 'I'll not be safe here if Tanner is around.'

'Where can you go?' Dorset asked. 'You have no relatives.'

Elena struggled to keep her voice calm. 'I feel certain that Captain Merrick is on his way to Natchez. I see no choice but to go to Natchez in the hope of finding him.'

Her announcement brought the reaction she was braced to encounter.

Dorset's chin dropped. 'You cannot!'

Hadley regarded her solemnly. 'Aye, Ma'am, it's no place for a lady. It's on the frontier.'

Elena was determined. 'I shall do this or perish in the attempt.'

'You have a home here,' Dorset said.

Elena rejoined, 'But that is all I have, Dorset. They've confiscated my accounts, everything. I cannot wait indefinitely. I'm not safe from Captain Tanner.'

Dorset persisted, 'But if the Captain comes . . .'

Interrupting her, Elena explained, 'Dorset, one of the deputies told me that Captain Merrick is aboard the *Sea Hawk* and they've sailed from Savannah.'

'Saints be! He's left you behind!'

'He had to,' Elena stated far more calmly than she felt. 'He might come back, but it could be months. He might not for a long time. It would be impossible to reach me here now. We have guards at front and back watching for him.'

'Perhaps that terrible Captain Tanner has left Savannah after him.'

'He may have,' Elena conceded, but she doubted it. She said, 'Every moment I'm here, I'm in danger from Captain Tanner. He's an old enemy of Captain Merrick's. They've fought at sea. He knows about the treasure and hopes to get it. I'm certain he expects I can lead him to the treasure.' She shook her head. 'I'm too vulnerable here. If I can just reach Natchez, I'll feel safe from that man. I feel certain I can find Captain Merrick.'

'But if you cannot . . . ?' Dorset murmured questioningly.

'I want to take that chance,' Elena stated. 'He'll get the trunks of treasure, then come back through Natchez. I have to try, Dorset. I'm in terrible danger from Captain Tanner. I must do this.'

'Suppose Captain Merrick returns for you?'

'If he does, it'll not be right away, but I don't think he will. I must get to Natchez.' She looked at both of them. 'The reason I've told you all this is to give you a choice. If you like, you may come with me. If you'd rather not, then I'll understand.'

Immediately Dorset spoke. 'If you must do this, Ma'am, I'll come along.'

Relief flooded Elena and she reached out to grasp Dorset's hand. 'Thank you, Dorset!'

Instantly Hadley added his desire to join them. Elena said, 'Thank you both. I'm so grateful. I'll see to it that you're rewarded for this.' Tears came to her eyes and she hugged Dorset.

The maid gazed at Elena. 'Miss, I've been with you since you were a babe. I cannot leave you now.'

Elena patted Dorset's shoulder. 'We must waste no time. Hadley, go down to the waterfront. See what you can learn about the *Sea Hawk*. Also, see if you can book passage on any ship bound for New Orleans. It may be months before we find one.'

'Suppose one is available and sails soon?'

For an instant Elena debated. Should she remain in Savannah on the chance that the *Sea Hawk* would return and Lance would come for her? She thought of Parnell Tanner's painful treatment. 'We'll leave whenever possible,' she answered. She crossed the room to a desk, opened it and removed a small chest which she handed to Hadley.

'Take this. If you do find a ship which will leave soon for New Orleans, use these coins to book passage for the three of us.' She glanced around the room. 'Before we go I'll sell what I can to raise funds for our journey.' She placed the chest in Hadley's hands, then looked up at him. 'Hadley, do be careful. Captain Merrick said that Parnell Tanner is an evil man.'

'Aye, Ma'am, I'll take care,' he replied and left.

As soon as he had departed, she gazed at Dorset. 'You might as well get some sleep, Dorset. This has been a dreadful night.'

'Aye, Ma'am. I'll stay with you.'

Elena shook her head. 'Go on to bed. I couldn't possibly sleep. I'll stay down here for a time.'

As soon as the door closed softly behind Dorset, Elena began to pace the floor. What a muddle everything had become! She moved to the window and gazed outside. Dawn revealed a thick fog obliterating all distant objects. Elena sighed and murmured softly, 'Lance!'

Where was he? Was he on the *Sea Hawk* sailing south towards the tip of Florida and then on to New Orleans? Or was he doubling back to Savannah to try and reach her? If only he could come take her away with him! She felt tears sting her eyes at the thought of his strong shoulders and fearless arrogance. All she wanted was to forget all her problems, be with her husband and know she was safe from the menace of Parnell Tanner.

It was over an hour later when Hadley reappeared. Dorset had come downstairs to talk to Elena when he knocked and entered the parlour. As he faced her, he wrung his hands and Elena realised that for the first time in her memory, the impassive man was distraught. Instantly, she feared he had encountered Tanner. When she asked, he shook his head.

'No, Ma'am. From all indications the *Sea Hawk* is on the high seas.'

Elena gripped the chair and closed her eyes. When Hadley coughed, she opened her eyes and looked at him. 'What else, Hadley? Will there be any ships bound for New Orleans or Louisiana Territory?'

He nodded. 'Aye, Ma'am. I booked passage for three on an ageing ship. It was the only one available and you instructed me to do so.'

She gazed at the tall, stoop-shouldered butler. Taciturn, with greying hair, he was utterly reliable. 'Thank you, Hadley. When does it sail?'

'Ma'am, you said to take whatever I could get. He hoists anchor in two hours . . .'

'Two hours!' she exclaimed.

Dorset gasped. 'You cannot go! Miss Elena, don't leave yet! Wait and see if Captain Merrick returns! Two hours is impossible!'

Two hours was an impossibility, Elena thought. How could she be ready that soon? Suppose Lance did return? She asked Hadley, 'Isn't there another ship that we can take at a later time?'

'No, none. Only the *Europa*. Captain Gotz will be out of the harbour two hours from now.'

'That's too soon,' she murmured.

'Do you want me to go back to see the Captain, Mrs Merrick? I can cancel the passage.'

Elena took a deep breath and shook her head. 'We'll go.'

'You cannot!' Dorset cried. 'Oh, Ma'am, it's a dreadful . . .'

Elena's response was simple. 'Dorset, I'm leaving. If you're coming with me, you'll have to hurry. We must take care in case Captain Tanner is watching this house.' She thought of all the things she had to do and the little time in which to get them done. 'We must pack. I'll take things we can sell to raise funds. I'll have to tell Mary and Jason and I have to tell the staff. Hadley, summon Perkins. I'll tell him that we should leave here in an hour and we must slip away without being observed.' She bit her lip as she tried to think of how to go and elude Tanner if he was watching.

'Hadley, when it's time to leave, tell Perkins to take the carriage to the Jacksons'. Dorset and I will go through the back ways and meet him there.'

'Aye,' he replied and left to fetch Perkins.

She turned to the maid. 'Dorset, pack your things, then come help with mine. Hurry, now!'

As if the heavens were in as great a turmoil as Elena's inner feelings, a storm boiled over Savannah's rooftops. Dark clouds swept over the town and gusts of wind whipped against Elena's cloak as she raced with Dorset to the Jacksons' for the carriage. Finally they were inside, rushing towards the bluff overlooking the wharf.

Elena twisted to peep at the street behind them. Her heart skipped a beat. She gasped and looked intently at the shadows. She felt certain she had glimpsed a rider and horse, but now they were gone. Was it imagination? Was it Lance? She dismissed that possibility. He was at sea. Also, he would not trail quietly behind. If he wanted her, he would come storming after her and carry her off with him.

When the carriage halted, Elena thought of Tanner. She pulled her cloak about her and stepped out as a bolt of lightning streaked across the sky. Grey stone steps led from the bluff down to the wharf, and she hurried down these to the ship.

With Dorset and young Perkins in tow, the three went aboard no proud schooner, but a cargo vessel that looked to Elena as if it belonged at the bottom of the sea. Captain Gotz was a burly man who apparently had little use for women on board, but was willing to take them for pay.

Elena was shown to a tiny, sparsely-furnished cabin which held only a bunk and built-in washstand. Dorset was given an even smaller cabin and Perkins was to bed down with the men.

It was dank and cold in Elena's cabin; a lantern swayed to and fro with the motion of the ship. Elena clutched the black woollen cloak tightly around her shoulders and paced the narrow area.

She heard shouts and feet pounding the deck overhead. Timbers creaked and she guessed they were moving out of the harbour. The Captain had asked her to remain below, but Elena could not resist the temptation to see what was occurring.

She ran up the narrow companionway to the deck, then remained in the shadows. The lights of Savannah flickered in the overcast dawn. The harsh glare of lightning illuminated steeples and chimneys, tall trees, masts and spars of ships at anchor, the dark grey water.

Where was Lance? Was he near Savannah—or was he headed for the Natchez Trace and his fortune?

Nearby a seaman shouted to another, causing Elena to jump with fright. She took a deep breath and gazed at the widening distance between ship and wharf. Lightning flashed and revealed the high bluff with grey stone steps leading down to the waterfront down which they had all hurried. Finally Savannah was lost from sight.

A strange, forlorn feeling enveloped her. She slipped below to her cabin and sat down on the bunk. She felt totally alone in the world. There was no one except Dorset and Perkins. She had left behind all friends and there was no family—except a husband. A husband in name only.

Elena lay down on the bunk and pulled the cloak close about her. She was chilled and miserable. She thought of Lance's strong, warm arms and how it had felt to be held close to his heart. She ran her hand across her eyes. How would she ever find Lance? Fright shook her and suddenly she wished she was back in her house at Savannah. Resolutely, she banished the thoughts and qualms. Her

decision had been made and there was no use looking
back.

Journeys by sea were notoriously lengthy and tedious,
but the morning finally came when she moved to the rail
to watch for the first sighting of New Orleans.

Sailing through boats filled with goods, the ship
headed for a dock. Elena gazed at the levee which
bustled with activity. Ahead stretched the low, flat town
of New Orleans.

Before she descended the gangplank, she looked in
amazement at the activity of stevedores, rivermen, and
peddlers. At the foot of the gangplank a melon vendor
pushed a cart filled with green fruit and proclaimed his
wares loudly in a sing-song call, 'Red-to-the-Rind! Red-
to-the-Rind!'

Fear overcame Elena. She knew nothing about this
land; for an instant she was frozen with fright and
uncertainty, but she forgot this the moment her loyal
servants joined her on the deck as they all prepared to
disembark.

They turned north and Elena gazed at the town established in 1718 by Jean Baptiste le Moyne, Sieur de
Bienville, governor of the French colony. An impressive
cathedral faced a *carré* or square, which was filled with
pink fuchsia, and white crêpe myrtle, oleander and
jasmine. Wide leaves of banana trees added shade.
Their carriage passed an open market with melons,
shrimp, crawfish, bananas, and pompano which whetted
her appetite.

With curiosity Elena studied houses which fronted
narrow walks. Black filigreed iron framed long second
and third floor galleries above the streets. They passed
the Cabildo, the government house built by the Spanish
when the French ceded the territory to Spain.

Some of Elena's fears were calmed when they located

an inn on Royal Street. Entering an arched door, they passed down a cool hallway which opened into an enclosed courtyard. A fountain sent splashing water into the air while scents of gardenias, camellias, and hibiscus added sweetness to the enticing odours of hot bread from a kitchen.

As soon as she reached the privacy of her upstairs room, Elena asked Dorset and Perkins to join her. She faced them to say, 'The sooner we depart for Natchez the better opportunity I'll have to locate Captain Merrick.'

She gazed at the two servants and realised that if she felt fear and uncertainty, they were even more fearful. Both were pale and lines of worry creased their faces.

Suffering a pang of sympathy, Elena patted Dorset's arm. 'Don't fret, either one of you. Captain Merrick may be in Natchez right now.'

Dorset voiced a question Elena had heard repeatedly from the maid since their departure from Savannah. 'Suppose he has already left Natchez and doesn't return?'

Patiently, Elena replied, 'If he goes back to Savannah, the Jacksons will tell him that we're in Natchez.' She straightened and said, 'Now, we must make haste to get ready before night falls.' She opened her reticule; her fingers brushed the map as she gathered coins to give to Perkins. She moved to the pile of their belongings and pointed to two portmanteaus. 'Perkins, sell everything and get what you can. We may have to reside in Natchez for some time.'

While he picked up the bags, Elena turned away. She could not bear to look at the silver serving dishes she loved and she knew sight of them would send Dorset into tears. She spoke stiffly, 'Acquire a wagon and team, Perkins, and sufficient provisions to get us from New Orleans to Natchez.'

'Aye, Ma'am.'

The moment he was gone, Dorset burst into tears. For the next hour Elena attempted to calm the maid's fears and banish her own. Later, when she lay in bed unable to sleep, she stared into darkness and trembled at the prospect of reaching Natchez and finding no trace of Lance.

She balled her fists and pressed them against her eyes. Where was Lance? It was impossible to guess what was in his thoughts when she was with him, doubly so now that they were separated. Firmly closing her mind to the perils facing them, she clamped her lips together and mentally went through the list of supplies Perkins had purchased.

It seemed she slept less than an hour, and by early morning they were on the first day's uneventful journey to Natchez. Inns were not so comfortable as in Georgia or New Orleans, but they seemed safe and adequate, for which Elena was thankful.

During the next five days they encountered travellers whose friendliness began to alleviate some of Elena's fears. On the last morning of their journey Elena expected to reach Natchez by late afternoon, but delays slowed their schedule. At mid-morning they halted to eat. When they paused beside the trail, the brief sight of a retreating bear so unnerved Dorset that it was longer than Elena had anticipated before they commenced travelling again.

During the afternoon their wagon wheels became imbedded in a soft creak bottom and required extra time to free them. While shadows lengthened across the trail, Elena grew tired. She drove the wagon, Dorset rode beside her and Perkins rode horseback. The land was flat, covered in brush and trees which became ominous in the gathering gloom.

Hearing sounds of other horses, Elena glanced at Perkins and said, 'Someone's coming.'

'Aye, Ma'am, I hear horses,' he replied, then two men rounded a turn and approached.

Dorset drew a sharp breath. 'They be bad'uns, Ma'am.'

'You don't know,' Elena admonished, but she shared Dorset's feelings. They halted briefly to talk with the strangers. Both men reeked of rum and wore tattered, dirty buckskins. They stated they had left Natchez about an hour earlier and asked Perkins questions about the Trace.

Wanting to see the last of the men, Elena and Perkins kept the conversation short, then turned the wagon ahead. As soon as the men rode out of sight, Perkins looked back over his shoulder.

For the next few minutes, Elena continually glanced at the empty trail behind them. Just as she was about to reassure Dorset that the men were gone, a commotion started on both sides of the trail.

Brandishing guns, two brigands burst out of the shadows to confront them.

CHAPTER
EIGHT

DORSET screamed and Perkins wheeled the horse around. A shot rang out and the young coachman pitched forward from his mount.

Elena scrambled down and rushed to him. To her relief he sat up and reassured her that he was all right. Belying his words, a dark stain appeared on his upper arm.

'You've been hit!' Elena cried.

Perkins waved a hand while Dorset knelt to tend the wound. Meanwhile, the brigands took possession of the wagon. As they started to go, Elena cried, 'You must leave us something!'

One of them snarled. 'You have a horse! Be thankful for that!'

They turned and urged the horses forward. Helplessly Elena looked after them as they disappeared ahead taking everything, except what she was wearing and one horse. She slipped her hand into a pocket and reassuringly touched the folded treasure map, then looked down at Perkins.

Hot tears streamed down her face and she knelt beside Dorset while the maid bound his injury. 'Perkins, this is my fault!' Elena cried. 'I shouldn't have brought you here.'

He attempted to quiet her. 'No, Ma'am. It was not your doing. It could have happened in Savannah with footpads.'

'You know it would never!' she cried. 'It's this terrible place!' She wiped her eyes with her sleeve and looked around. 'We must get you to a physician in Natchez.' Elena squeezed her fingers together. 'What will we do? We have nothing! There is nothing to pay for food or lodging. I have two sovereigns in my pocket.'

Perkins spoke firmly. 'I can find work, Ma'am. Don't fret.'

Elena said, 'Perkins, it should be only an hour to Natchez. Can you ride that far?

He nodded. 'Yes.'

She gazed at the horse; three people and one mount; what would they do? She sighed, 'Dorset, ride with Perkins and I'll walk beside you.'

Dorset straightened and her face grew red. 'I can't. I'll walk with you.'

Both women aided Perkins as he mounted, then they began the slow, tedious trek into Natchez.

With every step Elena's fears grew. How could they pay for anything? They needed lodging; Perkins needed medical attention and care. Her head swam with the horrendous problems facing them.

The air cooled and shadows closed in around them. Elena fought back tears. It would be useless to cry. She decided to sell the horse once they reached town; that would bring immediate funds, then she could work out what to do next.

The possibility that Lance Merrick might still be in Natchez was too welcome a thought to consider seriously. She dared not plan on finding him because she felt she could not cope with another disappointment. She was weary, frightened and hungry. Worse, she knew the others were more miserable than she and she was fully aware that when they did get to Natchez, she would have to make all the decisions. Resolutely determined that they would manage, she raised her chin and continued walking.

Half an hour later, in dusky early evening, her confidence wavered when they entered the oldest town on the Mississippi River.

Beneath high yellow bluffs on a crescent in the river were wharves fronted by jerry-built structures of logs. Saloons, taverns, and gambling houses flourished. River pirates, gamblers, flatboatmen, *Kaintucks*—as back-woodsmen from Kentucky and Tennessee were called—Indians, half-breeds and dance-hall girls milled together in Natchez-Under-the-Hill.

In a cluttered office above a saloon they located a physician, Dr Rogers. Reeking of ale, he treated Perkins' wound, informed Elena that it was slight, then suggested several places to stay. He agreed to allow Elena and Dorset to wait in his office while Perkins went to a livery stable and sold the horse.

As soon as he had returned, they paid the physician for his services and departed. Elena had learned that above the bluff was a respectable, growing town, but below was a wild, frontier port filled with wicked and dangerous activity.

With a weakened Perkins, the trio attempted to find lodging at a respectable inn on the bluff. When the innkeeper stated the sum for a night's lodging, Elena gazed at him in disbelief. She turned to Dorset.

The maid whispered, ''Tis almost all you possess.'

A knot came in Elena's throat. They had sold the horse, their only possession, Perkins was injured and unable to seek any temporary employment, and they had only a meagre sum. She thanked the innkeeper and motioned to the servants. Once they stepped outside, Dorset inquired, 'What will we do, Ma'am?'

'I asked Dr Rogers. There are places of lodging in Natchez-Under-the-Hill,' Elena replied grimly. She trudged along the dusty road which sloped away from streets lined with beautiful homes.

'We cannot!' Dorset cried. 'I saw those painted dance-hall women!'

'Dorset, that is the only place we can afford,' Elena explained. She glanced at Perkins. 'How are you feeling?'

'Well enough, Ma'am,' he replied evenly. 'Ma'am, as soon as we get settled, I'll commence searching for Captain Merrick. Miss Elena, I think I can bed down at the livery stable tonight.'

She smiled at him. 'Thank you, Perkins. We'll see.'

As they passed the first tavern, a gunfight erupted and Elena realised it was imperative to get lodging quickly. She took the first quarters they could find in order to have sanctuary. They climbed stairs to a sparsely furnished room which she shared with Dorset. Attic quarters were given to Perkins.

Gazing around the bare, dusty room with its sagging bed and cracked washbowl, Elena realised that even such poor shelter would cost more than they could afford unless they earned something within the next two days. She heard a noise and turned to discover Dorset with her hands over her face.

Elena patted her shoulder while Perkins shuffled his feet and cleared his throat. 'Ma'am, I'll make inquiries and see if I can locate Captain Merrick.'

Elena reached into a pocket and withdrew some coins to hand them to the young man. 'Perkins, do you feel able to do so?'

'Aye, Ma'am.'

'Please, be careful. I hate sending you out here at night, but we must attempt to find the Captain.'

'Indeed. Not to worry—I'll be all right.'

She shook her head. 'Perkins, I know your arm pains you. Get something for us to eat and wait until morning to search for the Captain.'

'I'll make a few inquiries, then return.'

'Perkins . . .' Elena hesitated. 'Take what you need and purchase a pistol. You're not safe without one.'

He faced her impassively and nodded. 'Aye.'

As soon as he was gone, she locked the door. Through the open window came the sound of a scream. Dorset sobbed loudly and Elena moved to the window to look below. Two men were locked in combat while a dancing girl stood in front of the door of a saloon and yelled at one of the men. More men milled about, a few called to the fighters. Perkins appeared and moved rapidly through the throng until he was out of sight.

Tears streamed down Elena's cheeks. How would they exist? They had money for only two days. After that, there would be no funds for food, lodging or anything. She would have to find employment—yet what could she do? If she sought a position as a maid in one of the fine houses on the bluff, it might take days. She had no equipment or talent for sewing, nor any place to do so.

No solution came to mind and she prayed that Perkins would find Lance. In a little over an hour the servant returned. He had purchased bread, cheese, a bottle of brandy, and apples. His face was grey and haggard and Elena knew that he needed rest.

She knotted her hands into fists and fought against disappointment when he told her that no one had heard of Captain Merrick. After dividing the food with Perkins, she said goodnight, then locked the door behind him.

Long after Dorset had settled on the creaking bed, Elena stood at the window and watched the activity below. Her gaze swept the boardwalk and she stiffened. Striding along with his back to her was a man with thick, black hair which curled over the neck of his buckskin clothing. His shoulders were broad and he was a head taller than other men he passed. Lance! For one fleeting instant that possibility made Elena's blood run hot and she thought what a relief it would be to have his strong shoulders on which to lean. The man turned.

All her hopes crashed. It was a stranger. Again and

again that night she glimpsed tall, dark-haired men. Even though she told herself that it could not be Lance, each time she peered intently until the man was lost from sight or turned to reveal an unfamiliar face.

Sleep was impossible; not until the first streaks of dawn did Elena doze in a chair. She awakened and stretched, then looked below.

In the early Saturday morning of the first of June, a hush settled over Natchez-Under-the-Hill. No one appeared anywhere along the street below. Boisterous, gaudy night life had vanished like a dream upon awakening. Utter stillness filled the air; there were no birds calls, no jingle of harness or clop of horses' hoofs.

Dorset rose, washed, then left to go to the attic to see how Perkins was. She returned with him, but Elena sent him right back to rest for the day. She smoothed her hair which she had fastened behind her head.

'Dorset, I intend to seek employment at one of the large homes on the bluff.'

'Oh, Miss Elena, never! Never can you do such a thing! I'll go!'

Elena answered calmly. 'I think we'll both go, Dorset.'

'Ma'am, you are a lady. You cannot do such labour!'

'Nonsense, Dorset.' She spoke kindly. 'It will do me no harm.'

Overwhelming Dorset's protests and reminding her of their few remaining provisions, the two women hurried up the road. By the end of the day, exhausted and more worried than ever, Elena returned with Dorset. Offering aid, people had fed them a substantial meal, but had not wanted their services on a regular basis.

When they reached their lodgings, Perkins was worse. Infection had set in. Dorset decided to sit with him which left Elena alone. Once again she sat by the window and gazed numbly below. What would they do when they could not pay for their rooms? She put her head in her hands and sobbed.

Finally she dried her eyes and sat up. Surely somewhere there would be a task she could do to earn her keep.

A tall, dark-haired man entered the saloon across the road, but Elena barely noticed. She knew it was not Lance. She bit her lip worriedly and watched as a dance-hall girl appeared in the saloon door.

Elena watched the dancing girl and her eyes narrowed. She drew a sharp breath, then jumped up and threw the black cloak around her shoulders. She closed the door quietly and raced down the stairs. If she stopped to think, she could not go ahead with her purpose.

She rushed across the street. The girl was no longer in sight, but Elena hurried around the corner of the saloon. Just as she hoped, there was a door in the back. She turned the knob and opened it to peer inside. No one was in view. She stepped inside, closed the door and moved in the direction of noise. The plank flooring was dusty and littered with rubbish. She reached an open door and heard two women's voices. Halting in the doorway to gaze at them tentatively, Elena said hello.

One had a mass of red-gold curls, the other had coal-black tresses. Heavily painted, wearing shocking dresses which revealed calf and ankle in daring black stockings, they looked at her with curiosity.

Elena learned the red-head's name was Maisie, the other Paula. While they listened, she poured out her troubles, omitting anything about the treasure, but stating that she was searching for her sea captain husband. Finally Elena paused to face them. 'I need a way to earn money. I have no more funds—I'm completely without any and I can't find work.' She took a deep breath and asked quickly, 'Can I dance?'

The two exchanged glances, then the red-head burst

into laughter. 'Go back up on the bluff where you belong, dearie!'

Paula giggled and shifted to study herself in a cracked mirror.

'Please,' Elena murmured.

'Go on with you!' Maisie stated and turned her back on Elena.

Elena gazed at them and saw her last hope dwindle. There was nothing left to do. She started to go, but hopelessness gave way to determination. She halted and looked at the two. 'You had to start sometime,' she stated forcefully.

Maisie regarded Elena in a long, silent study, then remarked, 'You'd faint when you got on stage, if you didn't faint, you'd burst into tears, your voice would quiver and your feet wouldn't move. You was meant for a saloon just about as much as I'm meant to live up on the bluff.'

'I can do it!' Elena protested.

Maisie frowned, then shrugged. 'Come here. Get on one of these dresses and we'll see Jack about it.'

Paula looked at Elena, then Maisie. 'Are you daft?'

Maisie shrugged. 'Give her a chance.'

'Jack won't let her on that stage,' Paula stated and turned around to smear rouge on her cheeks. 'He'll just take her home with him.'

Maisie's brown eyes rested on Elena. 'She's probably right.'

'I'll take the chance,' Elena replied, far more strongly than she felt.

Maisie looked at Elena. 'Then take off that dress.'

Elena did as she was told and shivered in the draughty room. Once Maisie began to help her, Paula joined them. They gave her a green satin dress which was two sizes too large. Paula spoke. 'Get that red satin. Ezzie were so tiny.'

Maisie handed it to Elena. Edged with black lace, the

low neck revealed her creamy skin. The bodice clung with an unnerving tightness to her tiny waist and hips, then the skirt flared in ruffles. Longer in the back, the front was cut to reveal her legs to her knees. Maisie poked through a box and handed Elena black stockings and garters.

As soon as Elena had pulled on the stockings, Maisie said, 'Now, take down your hair.'

When the golden strands tumbled over her shoulders, Paula's eyes grew round. 'Garamity! When Lil gets a gander of that, she ain't going to like it.'

Maisie smiled. 'Now, ain't that the pity.'

Realising there was more to Maisie's actions than merely aiding her, Elena asked, 'Who's Lil?'

'She sings,' Maisie stated. 'Go get Jack before Lil gets here.'

Paula nodded and left while Maisie pointed to a small barrel placed in front of the cracked mirror. An old table held an array of pots and bottles. Elena sat down and Maisie combed her hair away from her face, then pinned it high on both sides of her head allowing the golden curls to tumble down the back of her neck.

Carefully, Maisie began to apply powder and rouge to Elena's face. Elena closed her eyes and prayed that Dorset would spend the next few hours tending Perkins.

'This ain't the opera,' Maisie giggled. 'You won't have to do anything 'cept kick your heels,' she stated as she smoothed rouge on Elena's cheeks. 'Watch out for Lil. Just stay out of her way.' She looked at Elena and paused, 'Keep away from Jack, too.' For an instant Maisie's brown eyes softened. 'I got left by my man, just like you.' Her lips firmed and she urged, 'As soon as you earn something, get away from Natchez-Under-the-Hill—or you won't ever get out.' She glanced over her shoulder, then reached into the bodice of her dress and withdrew some coins which she pressed quickly into

Elena's hand. 'Here, take these. Get back to your room and out of here . . .'

Elena returned the coins and squeezed Maisie's hand. 'I couldn't take those, but thank you. You're so kind . . .'

Maisie blushed and reached for them again. 'You'd better go while . . .'

A voice sounded in the doorway. A short, broad-shouldered man appeared. Blond hair waved away from a tanned face. He snapped, 'What the hell is going on . . .' His gaze rested on Elena and he quit talking momentarily. With a brashness that embarrassed Elena he looked at her, then whispered, 'Holy harpers!'

'I figured you'd let her stay,' Paula remarked as she passed him and entered the small room.

Under his intense stare, Elena tried not to shiver. He strolled to her and tilted her face upward. 'What's your name?'

'Elena,' she answered.

''Lena,' he stated. 'You ever been in a dance-hall?'

She shook her head, but Maisie spoke. 'We'll teach her.'

He glanced at Maisie a moment, then looked at Elena. 'You're hired. I'll see you later tonight.' He turned to Maisie and Paula. 'She does all right, I'll give you a little extra.' He winked at them and left.

Maisie frowned, then continued to work on Elena. Three girls entered and Elena was introduced. One of them remarked, 'Lil's late. She's sozzled.'

A thin, wiry man appeared at the door. 'Time to go.'

Maisie poked Elena. 'Ready?'

Elena had been too engaged in meeting the newcomers to look at herself. She turned and looked at the stranger in the mirror. Powder and rouge made it almost impossible to recognise herself. With darkened lashes, her green eyes looked larger than ever. Her red lips were dry and she touched them with the tip of her tongue.

'Come on,' Maisie said.

She rose and followed the others from the room. Pressing clammy hands against the ruffles of her skirt, Elena felt chilled to the bone.

Close at hand all the dresses had patches, tiny tears and smudges. The building was in the same condition with rotting boards, trash and dirt. Noise and smoke assailed Elena. Loud notes of a piano added a false gaiety. How could she dance before a saloon full of rough frontier men?

Dizziness swept over her momentarily, but as it passed she glanced up to discover Maisie studying her. Maisie stepped to her side. 'You can still run for it.'

Elena shook her head. 'No, I won't.'

Maisie looked around, then leaned close. 'The moment Jack appears, demand pay for tonight, then get out of here.'

Elena nodded and Maisie continued, 'When we go on stage, just smile and kick your heels. Follow us. When I sing or does something you can't follow, get off stage, then come back. When we mingle with customers, you'll have to also.'

Elena gulped and squeezed her hands together. She had not considered mixing with the audience and it was too terrifying to contemplate. She halted beside Maisie behind a tattered curtain which partially hid them from view of the audience. Across the flickering glow of candles at the edge of the stage was a saloon filled with men.

Maisie motioned to Paula. 'Put her between us.' The girls placed hands on each other's shoulders to form a line, then Maisie quickly showed Elena the first few steps.

The curtain closed and immediately reopened, then they moved on to the stage. Elena fell into step, kicking her feet, attempting to keep up with Maisie and Paula.

Every moment was a nightmare. The dancing was

simple and easy to do, but Elena hated the leering men's faces on the other side of the candles. Above their heads smoke filled the air. Trying to ignore the raucous calls, Elena struggled to keep pace with the dancers. Maisie twirled past her and snapped, 'Lift your skirts more!'

Elena swished the flounces across her knees and tried to stare into space, then one by one each girl skipped forward to do a few solo kicks. Elena felt rooted to the boards. How could she dance alone and face all those men? Trembling, her knees felt weak.

In spite of efforts not to look at anyone, it was impossible to avoid glancing down. Boldly, men eyed her and called out suggestions Elena had never heard in her life.

Then it was her turn. Staring at the chandelier filled with candles which hung above the centre of the saloon, she skipped forward.

Her jaw ached from clamping it so tightly closed. She faltered and missed a step and a guffaw roared from the audience. Hot with shame, Elena raised her chin and kicked her foot. She glanced to one side and saw a bar filled with men, some watching her and a few turned away. With arms folded Jack regarded her. Her glance slid away, across tables filled with men, down the length of the bar.

Leaning over the bar facing the bartender, one of the customers turned to glance at the stage and his gaze met Elena's. Above the glowing tip of a cheroot the bluest eyes she had ever seen blazed with rage.

CHAPTER
NINE

LANCE! Elena could not move. She froze in shock and terror. Men began to yell, but all she saw was one man.

Shouldering everybody out of his way, Lance started for the stage.

As badly as she had wanted to find him, suddenly she was filled with fright. There was no doubt he was in a furious rage.

He shoved one man aside, then another swung at him. Lance smashed his fist into the man's jaw and continued towards her.

She could not take her eyes away from his fiery blue gaze. Maisie tugged on her arm and cried, 'Get off the stage . . .' Her voice trailed away as she asked, 'Do you know him?'

Releasing Elena, Maisie swore and ran. Fights had broken out in the saloon. At the piano a man played wildly in an effort to restore quiet.

Lance bounded across the candles. He stood before her and shouted, 'What the hell are you doing here?'

Without waiting for an answer, he swept her up into his arms and headed offstage behind the curtains. Elena locked her arms around his neck and buried her head in his shoulder.

When she felt cool air on her shoulders, she raised her head. They were outside, at the back of the saloon. Lance looked at her. 'Where are you staying?'

'Across the street,' she whispered. 'With Dorset and Perkins.'

'Damnation,' he muttered, then roughly dropped her

to her feet. His hands were on her waist and he looked at her. 'Why did you leave Savannah?'

'I had to find you. I wasn't safe there . . .'

He interrupted gruffly, 'Why wouldn't you be safe in Savannah?'

'Parnell Tanner broke in that night after I left.' She shivered and locked her fingers together. 'He threatened me with a knife . . .'

'Did he hurt you?'

'He was dreadfully frightening. He held a knife at my throat and demanded to know the location of the treasure. I lied about it and managed to get free by hitting him with a poker. Before he could do anything to me, Hadley and Perkins came to my rescue. He escaped that night, but I knew he'd return.'

Lance swore bitterly. 'Do you have the map?'

She nodded. Suddenly all her pent-up feelings began to surface. She threw her arms around him. 'Oh, Lance! It's been so terrible!'

His arms tightened around her. 'I don't know whether to kiss you or beat you!'

His arms felt like the only solid protection in a frightening world. She clung to him and sobbed. 'Lance, I'm so glad to see you!'

He shifted and held her away. 'We need to get out of here. Show me where you're staying.'

She looked down. 'I can't go anywhere in this! I left my dress and cloak inside.'

'You can't go back in there. Come on.'

She pulled against his hold on her arm. 'I have to. It's the only dress I own!'

He swore, but cautiously opened the door. Shouts and screams were heard. He slipped inside and Elena followed, then moved ahead to lead the way. 'Here,' she whispered and entered the empty dressing-room to snatch up her clothes. She looked around.

'Lance, this isn't mine. I need to change . . .'

'Like hell! We're getting out of this place while we can.' He took her hand and pulled her along behind him. They raced for the door. As they headed towards it, the man named Jack noticed them. He rushed to catch them.

'You! Hey! You're the cause of this!' Jack called. He reached out and caught her arm.

Lance turned and slammed his fist into Jack's jaw. Jack fell backwards hitting a stack of crates, then he slumped to the floor.

'Come on, Elena!' Lance took her hand and they raced through the doorway into the darkness. She hurried around the saloon while Lance threw the cloak over her shoulders.

Elena pulled it together to hide the red satin dress, as they passed a throng gathered in front of the saloon. A chair crashed through a window in a burst of glass. Shouts were loud and a gunshot roared above the noise. Elena rushed up rickety stairs to her small quarters.

To her relief, Dorset was not inside. She closed the door behind Lance and turned the key.

He glanced around. 'I thought you said Dorset and Perkins were with you.'

'They are. Dorset and I share this room and Perkins is in the attic. He's wounded and Dorset is with him.'

While she talked Lance went past her to the window and looked below. Elena studied him a moment. Clad in bucksin, his shoulders were stiff. A muscle worked in his jaw and his dark brows were drawn together.

'Why are you angry?' she asked.

He turned and looked at her. The rage she had noticed in the saloon had not completely diminished.

His voice was filled with controlled fury. 'Why were you on that stage?'

'I don't have a farthing.' Suddenly she could not bear his angry remoteness. She flung herself at him wrapping her arms around him. 'Thank heavens, you're here! I've been so terrified! Perkins was shot and we've been robbed.' Her shoulders shook as she sobbed, 'I hate it here! It's frightening and sinister . . .'

'It's just punishment for you, my little double-dealing wife!'

She sobbed against him. 'I don't care how angry you are with me. I'm so thankful you're here. Oh, Lance, how I wanted you! You're so strong. I can't bear this. Dorset and Perkins are like children. There's no money at all . . . I had to sell the silver, then everything was stolen from us . . .'

She poured out her troubles, then gradually realised how quiet he was. She wiped her eyes and looked up at him. 'Why are you so angry?' she whispered.

'I nearly lost my neck again, Elena, trying to get back to Savannah to bring my wife out with me!'

'Lance, I didn't know what to do . . .'

He interrupted, 'Elena, why do I doubt that? Your haste in leaving was spectacular. Once you had the map in hand . . .'

She straightened and said indignantly, 'How was I to know it would do me any good to sit in Savannah?'

He continued angrily, 'Your haste in leaving made me certain you would try to out-race me for the gold. I know your reasons for marriage. Now that I am quite healthy and alive,' he stated in a sardonic drawl, 'you are probably wishing you had not uttered those vows with me.'

She stiffened. 'You are a scoundrel, Lance Merrick!' Every time she was glad to see him, he said some cutting thing that broke her heart.

'Scoundrel?' he repeated. 'What an accusation, coming from a beautiful little mercenary who's willing to make any sacrifice for a trunk of gold.'

She started to move away, but his arms held her. 'Wait a minute, Elena,' he said in a tone that caused her to be still. He looked at her. 'How many people know the location of the trunks or that you have a map?'

'Only Dorset and Perkins know there is a treasure. No one has seen the map.'

He started to speak, but a tap on the door interrupted him, then Dorset called softly to Elena.

She pulled the cloak around her shoulders and unlocked the door. The moment it opened, Dorset gasped.

'Ma'am! What have you done to . . .' Dorset entered and saw Lance. 'Captain Merrick! Saints above!'

He greeted Dorset and inquired about Perkins. Casting a quick glance at Elena, Dorset said, 'He had a fever and his arm pains him a good deal.'

'I need to get you away from Natchez-Under-the-Hill.' Lance stated and looked at Elena. 'Get your things and I'll be back for you in an hour.'

As he moved to the door, Elena followed. 'Where are you going?'

He paused and looked down at her. 'I must get supplies, then I'll find lodging for the three of you, and then I'll be back to get you.' He glanced over her head at Dorset. 'Evening, Dorset,' he stated and took Elena's wrist to lead her into the hallway.

He gazed down at her solemnly. 'I'll be back shortly. In the meantime, don't leave this room. This is a dangerous place and you've made some enemies tonight.'

She nodded and watched him stride away. She wanted to talk to him, yet Dorset's presence prevented anything beyond polite conversation. Elena sighed, entered the room, and closed the door. She looked at Dorset and spoke quickly before the maid could ask questions.

'Dorset, we'll leave soon anyway; fetch Perkins and let him lie down here.'

'Aye, Ma'am.' Dorset left the room and Elena locked the door. As soon as she had changed from the red satin dress, she shoved it beneath the bed to hide it from Dorset. After scrubbing her face with cold water, she patted it dry and smoothed the skirt of her calico dress. Just as she was finishing, Dorset reappeared.

In a short time Lance returned. As he crossed the room to gaze at the sleeping Perkins, his boots clattered on bare planks. Studying his broad shoulders and firm jaw, Elena was filled with relief and joy that she had found him. She moved closer and whispered, 'Perkins keeps waking and dozing.'

Lance reached down to touch the man's shoulder. 'I'm going to wake him. I've found better lodgings and a physician to look at him.'

In less than an hour Lance had them settled in a pleasant inn above the bluff. Perkins had been visited by a physician and was resting in his room. Dorset had retired to her room and Elena faced Lance in her own cosy quarters.

Candles flickered and an oil lamp burned softly. Relief, joy, gratitude and excitement mingled in Elena. Now that they were alone, shyness enveloped her as she studied her new husband. He turned the key in the lock, then looked at her.

The angry blaze in his blue eyes startled Elena and she asked, 'You're still furious with me, aren't you?'

He answered savagely, 'I think I'm angry with myself for being such a fool.'

'I don't know what you mean.'

'You've always made it clear that you don't love me,' he stated. 'I should be able to resist.'

She could not follow his words. 'Resist what?'

'You.' He crossed the room and looked at her. 'You stay out of Natchez-Under-the-Hill and you'll be all right. Do you understand?'

She nodded. 'Why are you telling me this? You sound as if you won't be here with me.'

'That's right, Elena. I'm leaving now.'

'Leaving! Where are you going?'

'I intend to fetch those trunks.'

'Can't you send somebody for them? You can't go alone.'

'I've spent my last dollar to keep the three of you here while I'm gone. I came out of Savannah with two of my ships. Some of my men should share in the buried treasure, instead, I gave them my ships and their cargoes. I've used my funds to purchase necessary items for the trek along the Natchez Trace.' He placed a small leather bag on a table. 'Here's sufficient to buy food while I'm away.'

His revelations shook Elena. 'You have nothing if you lose those trunks.'

He spoke evenly. 'That's right.'

As if to reassure herself as well as Lance, she stated, 'The trunks are there and filled with all you could hope for!'

'And that's why I'm going.'

'You're in a rush,' she stated stiffly. Hurt and dismay filled her. If Lance lost the trunks . . . the prospect was too horrible to consider.

An eyebrow arched and he regarded her intently. 'Do you want me to stay until morning?'

The question hung in the air. Did she want this angry man to stay? She looked at the husband who was almost a stranger.

He turned away. 'Never mind, Elena.'

'Lance . . .'

He paused and gazed at her with glacial blue eyes. He said, 'I'll save you the trouble. I can't stay even if you wanted me to.'

'Why not?'

'You said Parnell broke into your house.' He paused and she nodded. He continued, 'Then he's followed you to Natchez.'

'That's impossible! I haven't seen him once.'

Lance insisted, 'He's followed you. I've made inquiries in the last hour. It's not difficult to discover if

Parnell is in town. If I leave now, I just might lose him. Also, I'll have a head start if he wrings the map from you. He won't expect me to leave you this night.' His voice was filled with bitterness. 'He'll expect me to spend it with my new bride.'

'Lance . . .'

He continued relentlessly, 'If I can get a head start, that's all I'll need.'

She crossed the room to catch his sleeve as he reached for the doorknob. 'Lance, you can't leave when you're so angry. What have I done?'

He turned and looked down. Fire flashed in his eyes and he spoke with restraint. 'I told you, Elena, you left me to risk my neck to get back to Savannah while you made a run for the gold. If you hadn't been robbed, don't tell me you wouldn't have hired someone by now to seek the trunks.'

'That's not so!' she exclaimed.

He stood only inches away. Her hand lay against his arm and she felt the tight muscles beneath the buckskin. She looked at him and moistened her lips while her anxiety increased.

'Damn you!' he whispered suddenly and swept her into his arms for a searing kiss. He crushed the breath from her lungs, but his kiss was not harsh; it was passionate, hungry and fiery. Her willing body moulded against the length of him. She closed her eyes and clung to him.

With startling swiftness he released her and was gone. She yanked open the door and called to him, 'Lance!'

He turned the corner to descend the wide stairs and was out of her sight. Elena knew it would be useless to chase him. She closed the door and leaned against it. She felt drained, exhausted from all the turmoil. He was taking a dangerous trail, the Trace, the *Devil's Backbone*, alone.

He could be in dreadful danger. If something hap-

pened to Lance—Elena bit her lip with worry. She began
to pace the floor. How could she stand waiting day after
day for him to return, staying in the inn with Dorset and
Perkins and wondering what had happened on the
Trace?

An idea began to form. She would go alone! Elena
knew that was what she wanted to do. She snatched up
the bag of coins and opened it, then sighed with relief.
There was sufficient to procure a horse for her and still
be certain that Dorset and Perkins would be all right.

She unlocked the door and went to Dorset's room to
waken the maid. When Dorset learned her decision, she
exclaimed, 'Ma'am, you can't go after him! Look at the
folly this has been . . .'

'Dorset, he can't be far ahead and he's on the Trace.
Get the innkeeper and ask him to purchase a horse for
me and ask him to get a boy's clothing.'

'I cannot!'

'Indeed, you can,' Elena replied. 'Now hurry!'

'Suppose you miss him—or can't find him—or meet
brigands first?'

'I won't if you'll hurry, Dorset. I won't listen to this
foolishness. Please, go. Time is essential!'

As soon as Elena received the clothes, she dressed
with feverish haste. Ignoring Dorset's pleas, Elena
braided her hair and wound it around her head, then
studied herself in the mirror. She looked like a sixteen-
year-old youth—a rather unmanly one with full red lips
and rosy cheeks. She pulled a wide-brimmed hat over
her hair. Boots added to her stature. Her white shirt and
black breeches fitted snugly, but Elena was satisfied that
a cursory glance would give a stranger the impression of
facing a lad. She gathered up the map, the pistol Perkins
had purchased, a powder horn and gloves. As she
worked, Dorset began to cry.

''Tis the worst folly,' she murmured.

Elena threw the dark cloak around her shoulders and

hugged the maid. 'Shh, Dorset. We'll be back before long. I'll take care. If I don't catch up with him tomorrow, I'll turn around and come back by dark.'

'Promise?' The maid's voice quavered.

'Yes. It's a promise.' Elena hugged her again, then slipped from the room. She hurried downstairs, had a brief final word with the innkeeper and listened carefully to his instructions on locating the Trace.

Once she was mounted, she kept to the shadows. A bright moon shone clearly, but Elena wore a black cloak and rode a dark horse. Every few minutes she twisted and looked all around.

She tried to remain calm and not dwell on the fact that Parnell Tanner was somewhere close at hand. As she rode quietly along, she passed houses which reminded her of New Orleans. Two-storied, of red brick and flush with the street, galleries grilled with fancy iron work.

Once she left town, she led the horse along the edge of the Trace. She realised there was more to Natchez than she had first surmised. Not only were there lovely homes above the bluff, but she passed several mansions that were as beautiful as any she had ever seen.

Within a short time the Trace wound beneath a high bank. Above it was an inn. Made of timber and whitewashed, below a steeply sloping roof it had two long galleries supported by nine colonnettes. Elena led the horse beside a window, then rose in the saddle to peer inside for any sign of Lance.

There were only four men sitting at a table. Her husband was not among them. She slipped down and rode back to the Trace to continue her journey.

Something crunched behind her and Elena turned quickly. She peered into the darkness, but could not discern anything. She led her horse into the trees and halted while she listened. The longer she waited, the more menacing the night became.

Finally she urged the horse forward. Soon the wide

Trace began to narrow, twisting and winding through a forest, until it became a tangle of vegetation and Elena was afraid she would lose the way.

Small rustlings could be heard; the forlorn call of an owl sent a chill through her. Around Savannah the sight of oaks draped in Spanish moss had appeared graceful, but on the lonely Trace trees and moss became ghostly and frightening.

Gazing into the inky darkness beneath spreading oaks, Elena could believe Lance's tales of people disappearing along the Trace. If something happened along this trail, who would know?

She began to regret her decision to attempt to catch Lance, yet the thought of turning around and travelling alone to Natchez was worse. She kept continually reassuring herself that somewhere ahead was Lance.

She studied her surroundings. How little wealth and position would matter here, she thought. It was the place for someone like Lance—he was exceedingly strong and quick-witted.

The Trace widened and she urged the horse to a faster pace. Lance could not be too far ahead. He would have left Natchez quietly without undue haste in an effort to avoid attention. Something stirred close at hand and Elena looked over her shoulder.

She tugged the reins and slowed the horse so they would not make such a disturbance. Again, she heard something, but once more she could detect nothing definite.

Frightened, she opened the saddlebag a fraction and touched the cold barrel of the pistol. She heard the sound of gurgling water, coming from the stream which poured across the Trace just ahead of her.

Elena dismounted to allow the horse to drink. She moved into the shadows and gazed around. A twig snapped. Suddenly arms closed around her like bands of steel.

CHAPTER
TEN

WHILE her heart pounded wildly, she gasped and struggled.

'Why are you following me?' a familiar voice whispered in her ear.

'Lance!' she murmured and felt limp with relief.

'What the devil?' Shoving her into a patch of moonlight, he turned her to face him.

'Dammit! Elena, what are you doing here!' He yanked the hat off her head and gazed at her with an angry scowl.

'Lance, I couldn't stay behind in Natchez. I've been trying to catch up with you. I left shortly after you did.'

In a steady, level tone, he swore. 'You probably just led Parnell Tanner right to me!'

His anger shook her. 'I tried to be careful when I left Natchez.'

'I ought to send you right back there . . .'

She clutched his arms. 'Oh, no! Lance, I can't sit in Natchez and wait and not know what's happening. I may be able to help you in some way . . . please, you can't send me back.'

He rubbed his brow and muttered, 'No, I can't. C'mon, let's get out of the moonlight to discuss what we'll do.'

He gathered her horse's reins, mounted, then lifted her easily before him. Elena remembered the first night she had met Lance and how they had ridden together. Memory was crowded out by his voice.

He remarked softly, 'I can't take you back, Elena. If I

return to Natchez, I'll never have a chance to get to the trunks.'

'Then you'll have to let me stay,' she said.

'Aye, that I will.'

'How did you know I was following you? I didn't realise you were anywhere close.'

'I'd stopped to rest and heard someone, then I doubled back and followed you for a way.'

'You've been following me!' She thought of all her fears. During that time Lance had been close at hand. She sighed. 'If only I'd known.' She asked, 'How did you know I wasn't just another traveller heading home?'

'I didn't. If that had been the case, I'd have released you, apologised, and gone away.'

Her nerves were frayed and she longed for his laughter, his reassuring strength. She twisted to look up at him. 'Lance, you mustn't be angry with me because I left Savannah. I didn't know when you'd return or if you could. The High Constable searched the house, then posted men at the doors to watch for you. I had no way of knowing you would come back.'

'So you said, Elena,' he answered, then, 'Keep your voice down. I'm going to dismount. Keep on riding. I won't be far behind and I'll catch up with you. Don't go any faster than we are now.'

'Why?'

'I think someone is following us.'

His words filled her with cold fear. 'I know I didn't lead Captain Tanner out of Natchez! I was so careful . . .'

'Shhh,' he cautioned. 'Elena, you know nothing about tracking in a wilderness. You had no idea I was behind you until you felt my arms around you.'

'Lance, Tanner can't be near!'

'Now keep right on,' he instructed and slipped off the horse.

Elena wanted to look back, but she resisted the

temptation. Suddenly the night seemed filled with even more menacing danger than it had before.

In the distance she heard an eerie, forlorn howl. Each time it was repeated, Elena wanted to cover her ears. If Lance was correct and Captain Tanner was following . . . what would they do? She clamped her lips together and tried to listen for Lance. All night there had been rustling noises around her, but she still could not discern any indication that Lance was near.

He emerged in front of the horse to her right so suddenly that she had to bite back a scream. He mounted easily and reached around her to take the reins.

When he remained quiet, she turned and looked up at him. 'Did you find anyone?'

Grimly, he answered, 'Somebody's there. My guess is Tanner.'

She shivered. 'Lance, I didn't dream I'd lead him to you.'

He looked down and stated softly, 'Stay alert now. If you see or hear anything out of the ordinary, any little thing—let me know at once.'

When she remembered Tanner's harsh treatment in Savannah, she doubled her fists and stiffened. Realisation that he was somewhere in the dark behind them, waiting to destroy them for the gold, unnerved her. Her mouth felt dry and she longed for town and civilisation. 'I shouldn't have come,' she whispered.

'It's too damn late for regrets,' he remarked. He shifted and dropped to the ground.

'Where are you going?' she asked in alarm.

'Wait a minute. My horse is here.' He climbed a bank to one side of the Trace and moved out of sight, then returned in a minute astride a black horse. He was leading another horse which carried supplies.

She asked, 'Will we ride all night?'

He looked at her. 'Are you tired?'

'No! How could I think of sleep out here?' She glanced at him and saw moonlight glint on the grey barrel of a pistol. 'What are you doing?'

'I just don't want to be surprised,' he answered evenly.

They rode in silence and Elena knew he was still angry. She could now understand his fury, particularly in leading Tanner to him. She wished now that she was back in Natchez, but the moment she acknowledged the thought, she realised she would rather be with Lance and know what was happening.

She reached across a narrow space and touched his arm. 'Lance, I'm sorry. I tried to be careful when I left town.'

'Forget it, Elena. There's no looking back.' He urged his horse ahead and rode in front of her.

Elena gazed at his broad shoulders and wondered what kind of marriage they would ever have. Behind her something crackled and Elena turned quickly to peer through the trees.

She looked at Lance, who had also turned. He merely shrugged.

The first time they halted to rest, dawn had brightened the Trace. Kneeling beside a stream, Elena splashed cold water on her face. Lance moved downstream out of sight, then shortly returned. He reached into a saddlebag and brought out a loaf of hard bread and a packet of dried meat.

He produced a bottle of ale and said, 'I don't want to stop long or build a fire. We'll have a better meal tonight.'

Elena ate little of the dreadful breakfast, then soon mounted and rode beside him. Twice during the day they met travellers heading south along the Trace.

By late afternoon Elena was hungry and tired. Determined to keep pace with him, she bit back any protests, but was thankful when he finally halted.

Lance dismounted and said, 'Before the last glimmer of light is gone, I want to find a meal and gather twigs for a fire.'

'Won't that be dangerous?'

He shrugged. 'Since Tanner didn't accost us last night, I don't think he will until I've led him to the treasure. He'll bide his time.'

Elena received the news with mixed emotion. Momentary relief filled her, yet at the same time, Lance's words carried a finality that sounded like a threat of absolute doom. Dismounting, she expressed her feelings, 'At least we won't have to watch all night.'

Lance's hand dropped over her wrist. Startled, she looked up at him. He said, 'Elena, don't ever let down your guard while we're on this Trace.'

The threat seemed to be one too many bits of bad news. 'This is so frightening . . .' Her voice faded as she glanced down the Trace.'

'But not sufficiently frightening to prevent you from coming to get the gold,' he commented dryly.

Her nerves were frayed and his jibe stung. She locked her fingers together. 'I couldn't bear to wait in Natchez and not know what was happening. I thought you might need me . . .' The anger that flared in his blue eyes caused her voice to falter.

'You can't wait to get your fingers on that gold, Elena!'

His fury touched a spark in her and she raised her chin. 'Lance, I have nothing because of you! I had a normal, peaceful life, wealth, a fiancé, until you came to Savannah! I am penniless now!' She added, 'I did think you might need another person. I forgot how self-sufficient you can be.'

He drawled sardonically, 'I'm delighted to have my wife at my side. After all, Elena, we have all these nights together, sleeping under the stars in one of the most beautiful places in this territory.'

She blanched and stepped away from him. 'You're not to touch me, Lance Merrick!'

He looked down at her. 'After our vows, Elena, I told you, I'll touch you whenever I damn please.' He reached out and pulled her to him.

'Stop it!' she cried. 'You don't feel any love . . .'

His mouth silenced her objections. Elena stood stiffly in his embrace. She was filled with fear and anger and had no desire for his kisses.

Insidiously, he drove each emotion away. First, fear was diminished and forgotten, as all surroundings were obliterated, driven out by two warm hands and a hard lean body. Then the coolness she felt towards him fled; it evaporated in a mist of increasing desire that swirled through every part of her being.

Unbelievably, against her wishes, in a time and place where she would have thought it impossible to relax and forget danger, this man was driving out everything except desire for him.

Suddenly he released her and looked at her. His chest heaved with ragged breathing and his voice was hoarse as he stated flatly, 'We'll lose our chance to build a fire if we don't do so soon.'

Through lowered lashes she gazed up at him. He looked at her intently, then turned abruptly and went to work gathering logs. She gazed at his back, the narrow tapering waist and hard, muscled legs. Why had he stopped? Was it because of the fire—or something else?

She sighed and began gathering twigs. Lance readied his pistol and she asked, 'What are you doing?'

'Going to find dinner. I'll return shortly, Elena. Fire a pistol if you face any danger. I have an extra one in my saddlebag . . .'

'I brought one,' she said.

He nodded and was gone from sight in an instant. Dark shadows beneath the spreading branches of the trees swallowed up all trace of him. Ghostly fronds of moss moved gently with the breeze and Elena shivered.

Hurriedly, she worked to build a fire, attempting to shut away all consideration of danger. Within minutes she heard a shot and Lance returned bearing a sizeable, ugly oppossum.

She gazed at it and shuddered. 'You're a barbarian, Lance. You may keep that for yourself.'

'Certainly, Elena,' he replied good-naturedly, then retrieved a tinder-box from his saddlebag and commenced to light the pile of logs and brush.

Elena wanted none of the unappetising meat, but after it began to roast, succulent smells filled the air.

Finally, when he began to cut slices of browned meat, she asked for some.

He laughed. 'Ah, so possum will meet your standards.'

'It does smell enticing.'

After cutting some for her, he produced the flagon of ale from his saddlebag and sat down on a blanket beside her. She glanced around. 'Lance, are there Indians here?'

'They may travel the Trace, but the Natchez tribe is gone. They were north of here. Years ago in a battle with the French, they were almost wiped out. Those who survived were driven away. Their chief was considered a sun god; they carried him in order to keep his feet from touching earth.'

With emphasis, Lance added, 'He had absolute control over others in the tribe, particularly his wives.'

'You'd like that,' she stated.

He glanced up. 'No, Elena, it's not control over you that I want.' He paused a moment before he continued, 'When the Natchez chief died, his wives were strangled to accompany him on his journey in another life.'

'How cruel!'

'Maybe. Anyway, all of them are gone from this area.

Survivors have been driven westward to join other tribes.'

Elena shivered. Lance stood and picked up two heavy logs to place on the fire. She rose to help clear away the remnants of dinner while he fetched a rolled blanket.

A high wail pierced the night and Elena stiffened. 'What was that?' she whispered.

Lance answered calmly, 'Most likely a wildcat.'

'This wilderness is terrifying.'

Lance spread the blanket near the fire, sank down and motioned to her. 'Come here, Elena.'

Another shrill howl sent her willingly beside him. He pulled her close and sat back against a tree.

She gazed around. 'Will fire keep wild animals away?'

'We'll be safe,' he replied. She glanced down and noticed that two of the pistols were within reach on the other side of him.

The fire crackled and sparks shot upwards into the night. The warmth and brightness of the flames were reassuring.

Pine logs filled the air with a tangy aroma. Elena straightened and held her hands towards the flames.

'Cold?' he asked.

'Not really, but it feels nice.' She felt his hands touch her head as he removed her hat, then unfastened the long, yellow braid. He began to unplait her hair until it was free and covered her shoulders in golden waves. An owl hooted in a long, hollow sound and Elena turned to Lance.

'I don't know what I would have done if I'd missed you,' she stated.

'I suspect you would have muddled through some way,' he replied. He drew her against his chest.

Warmed by the hot meal and flagon of ale, weary from the long ride and frightening night, Elena felt exhausted. For the first time since they had landed in New Orleans, she could relax. Bone-weariness filled her and she settled in his arms. She leaned her head against the rough buckskin covering his chest and listened to the deep, steady heartbeat.

In a moment a rumble of laughter roused her and she looked up sleepily. 'Are you laughing, Lance?'

She realised he was and sat up to study him. It was the first time she had heard him laugh since Savannah. 'What do you find amusing?'

'I'm laughing at myself and what you're doing to my male pride.'

'I can't be doing anything to it! You're far too arrogant to suffer.' She hid a yawn and settled into the hollow of his shoulder.

He kissed her temple and spoke in an amused drawl. 'Go to sleep, Elena.'

A thought occurred and she looked up at him. 'Lance, are you ever afraid of anything?'

Laughter died and he became solemn. 'Only one thing, Elena. Go to sleep—at the moment I'm not about to tell you what I fear.'

She could not discern his reply, but she was too weary to make an attempt. She closed her eyes and placed her head against him.

During the night she awakened to gaze into darkness. Disorientated and confused, she peered at a stream of grey smoke rising from twinkling embers. An arm tightened around her and she glanced quickly at Lance.

She was held tightly beside him while she stretched against the length of his body. Somewhere nearby an animal rustled the undergrowth. Elena shivered and pressed closer against Lance.

The next time she opened her eyes, Lance was up tending a fire. He directed her towards a stream and she left to wash. When she returned, she found Lance had cooked a small pigeon and was ready to eat. She joined him to sit on a blanket and ask, 'How many days until we reach the trunks?'

'Not many,' was his vague reply. 'Elena, from time to time, I may drop out of sight, but I'll be behind you. You lead the extra horse today.' He regarded her and added, 'You should braid your hair again. You'll attract less notice and be safer.'

Without argument, she did as he instructed and soon they were on the Trace heading north. Within a short time she was listening for hoofbeats. If she did not hear them, she would glance around for sight of him.

Periodically, Lance was out of view. Each time, Elena felt more vulnerable, yet it was not as disturbing as it had been when she was alone. Back there somewhere was Lance and she was reassured.

Midday they halted to eat bread and dried meat and drink the ale which he had brought in his saddlebag. Refreshed, they commenced the ride again and within the hour encountered another wagon carrying two men who were headed south.

For a quarter of an hour they exchanged pleasantries. Both men answered Lance's questions about conditions on the Trace, then they said farewell and continued.

Late in the afternoon, Lance rode up and asked, 'Tired?'

She nodded. 'A little.'

He smiled. 'We'll halt soon.' Within the hour he turned the horses and they mounted an incline to halt beneath tall oaks. Lance produced his pistol and instructed her, 'You gather wood for a fire, Elena, while I get dinner.'

She did as he asked and by the time he returned with a wild turkey, she had built a roaring fire. Soon the bird was roasting; while it cooked, Lance rearranged supplies and unrolled a stretch of canvas. Elena asked what he was doing.

He glanced overhead. 'It's impossible to see through branches here, but earlier I noticed fish-scale clouds. We'll need shelter if it rains.'

Finally they ate and the turkey was delicious. Elena's spirits lifted. The fire was cosy and warm, their day had been peaceful and she was no longer so fearful. Even Lance's opinion that they were being followed by Parnell Tanner failed to dampen her good humour. She scoured utensils in a stream and returned them to a saddlebag. When thunder rumbled in the distance, she looked at Lance.

'You were right; it's going to rain.'

He shrugged. 'Perhaps. It's far away at the moment.' He spread a blanket before the fire, sat down and patted a place at his side. 'Come sit with me, Elena.'

She did as he asked and he drooped his arm around her shoulders to pull her against him. For a moment they gazed at the fire in silence. Logs he had just heaped on smouldering embers caught on fire. A tongue of orange scorched the rough pine bark and sent an appealing aroma into the air.

Elena felt contented and at peace. She looked down at Lance's hand tracing circles on her arm. Along his wrist black hairs sprang away to disappear beneath the edge of a buckskin shirt. After a moment she leaned forward and wrapped her arms around her knees while she gazed at the crackling logs.

Lance reached up and commenced to work loose the braid around her head. He asked, 'Are you tired?'

She nodded. 'Yes. When I close my eyes I feel as if I'm still on horseback.'

He shifted forward and began to rub her shoulders. Elena closed her eyes. Massaging all weariness away, his hands were warm and gentle.

Shortly she grew aware that his touch had changed. Lightly, with languorous deft strokes, his hands no longer soothed, but sent disturbing waves of feeling through her.

He lifted heavy, golden tresses and kissed the nape of her neck while his finger traced the curve of her spine.

It was impossible to ignore or resist. She twisted to wrap her arms around his neck.

Eagerly he gathered her into his arms. He laid her on the blanket beside him while he kissed her hungrily.

Throbbing desire consumed her. In that moment, Elena was certain that all the gold they were after would never give her the thrill that a mere embrace by Lance could.

He was a renegade, a pirate, yet so gentle that his caress was a silky touch. Like rippling waves rising to crest and crash, his caresses stirred a longing which heightened and rose, then flooded her.

As if consumed by the same hunger, he began to peel away barriers of clothing. Her black coat was discarded. He tugged at her coarse white cotton shirt, then drew it over her head to expose smooth, golden skin covered by a thin chemise. His buckskin shirt was tossed aside.

Elena ran her hands over the bronzed muscles of his shoulders, then across smooth skin until she stroked a tiny ridge of flesh along his shoulder blades. Her eyes opened in surprise and she looked up at him.

She pulled away slightly and ran her fingers along his spine. 'Lance . . .' Beneath her hands she discovered a row of ridges. She sat up. 'Lance, your back . . .' Elena shifted to gaze at his broad shoulders and muscular back which narrowed to a small waist. Criss-crossing coppery skin were thin, white scars which caused her to gasp. She asked, 'What happened?'

He pulled her into his arms again, and looked down at her. 'I didn't want to go to sea.' He shrugged. 'I was hot-headed and determined to get free. It earned me floggings.'

'I'm so sorry,' she murmured.

He unwrapped her arms and looked at her piercingly. ''Twas in the past and over.'

Solemnly, she gazed at him. 'How can you smile?'

His voice was light and he trailed his fingers along her

arm. 'Because, my hot-blooded little minx, you're far more soft-hearted than I guessed.' He picked up her hand and gazed at the crude ring he had fashioned, then looked at her.

'I expected this to be discarded long before now.' He lowered her hand and his voice deepened as he whispered, 'You're the most beautiful woman in the world!'

Elena flushed from his appraisal and his compliment. His arm slipped around her waist to draw her to him. With a surging insistence his mouth possessed hers.

He lowered her to the blanket and she felt his weight come down on her while he kissed her passionately.

Suddenly he rolled away and flung a blanket over her. 'Pull on your clothes, Elena, then we'll move closer to the fire.'

Startled, she frowned at him. 'Why? Lance . . .'

'Do as I say.' His voice was so rough that she feared not to. Hurriedly she tugged on the shirt, then her coat. She rose and moved towards him.

He pulled the buckskin shirt over his head. A few feet away from him Elena halted. 'Lance.'

He turned to face her; a harsh scowl lined his features. She crossed to him and placed her hands against his chest. She whispered, 'Why did you stop?'

He smoothed hair away from her forehead. His voice was low as he replied, 'I want you to have a church wedding and a beautiful dress.'

She turned away quickly and moved to stand in front of the fire while he sat down on the blanket nearby. Once she was away from him, she was not certain what she wanted. In the distance thunder rumbled again and a gust rippled branches overhead.

Lance patted the blanket and she moved to sit beside him. He whispered, 'Also, Elena, we are not alone.'

She stiffened. She had completely forgotten Parnell Tanner, any danger or prying eyes. Waves of embarrassment and anger engulfed her.

'Lance Merrick! You knew that all the time!' She quivered with indignation and had to fight temptation to look searchingly into the darkness surrounding them.

She glared at him. 'Lance, you can be the most infuriating person!' A streak of lightning caused her to jump.

Lance looked up. 'We will have rain soon.' A cold gust of wind whipped tops of trees and whistled through the branches as another jagged streak of lightning illuminated the forest. He placed his arm around Elena's shoulders. 'Come closer, Elena.'

She snuggled against him and murmured, 'I hate storms.'

Suddenly the first big drops of rain struck. Lance jumped to his feet and dashed to get the canvas. He placed it on the ground, pulled her down beside him and tugged a large piece of the canvas over their heads while Elena pulled the blanket over them.

He looked down at her. 'This isn't so bad.'

She listened to the thunder and put her head against his chest. After a moment she looked up and asked, 'When will we reach the trunks?'

'Perhaps tomorrow.'

'What will you do about Tanner?'

His voice hardened. 'I will have to be ready. Once we get the trunks, he will make his move.'

His answer chilled her. Lightning flashed and made a sharp crack; they heard a splintering and a tree limb crashed.

Elena closed her eyes and clung to Lance. After a few moments she felt him brush a tendril away from her cheek. She relaxed and yielded to exhaustion.

The next thing she knew Lance was calling her name. 'Elena, wake up. We should be on our way.'

He leaned down to kiss her lightly. Quickly he straightened and pulled her to her feet.

She stretched and yawned. 'I must have slept soundly.'

He grinned. 'You did. The rain stopped right after you fell asleep. I'm doing some cooking now.'

After they had eaten a warming breakfast of roasted woodcock, they commenced the trek. In a few miles they reached a point where it had not rained and the ground was hard. The land was flat, dense with trees and undergrowth. Through trees to the east, Elena caught glimpses of water.

During midday Lance reined and pointed towards a large, splintered oak. Beside it was a jagged stump. 'Here's where we leave the Trace,' he stated.

Peering in the direction he faced, Elena saw a shadowy area of moss, trees and bushes. A premonition of disaster halted her. As Lance moved ahead, she gazed carefully around, then followed.

Little sunlight broke through the canopy of oak leaves and Elena noticed the ground was dotted with tiny pools of water.

Lance dropped back to ride beside her. He spoke softly. 'We'll dig up one trunk, Elena, and take sufficient gold to allow us freedom, then return to Natchez. By riding at a fast pace, we can be back in Natchez in a short time. We'll have enough gold to allow you to wait in comfort while I bring some men and return for the rest of the trunks.'

She saw the wisdom in his plan, but wondered about Captain Tanner.

Within minutes each hoofbeat made a tiny splash. In the distance the terrain looked solid, but the horses stirred water that sent ripples through the grass. Soon they neared the edge of the trees. Elena urged her horse forward to ride beside Lance.

The trees thinned and she gasped at the view. 'Lance!'

They had reached an expanse of open water surrounded in the distance by trees. Sunlight shimmered on the glossy surface. It looked like a vast lake; the only indication of its shallow depth was a large clump of grass and a decaying log jutting out of the water.

With a flapping noise a white heron settled. Judging by the depth of water on its long legs, Elena saw that the lake was quite shallow.

She rode beside Lance while they crossed the lagoon. When she spotted a mudbank to her right, she asked, 'Lance, would it be better to travel there?'

He looked in the direction she had pointed. 'No, Elena. Some is mud and sand, but there is quicksand. We are safer here.'

'What is quicksand?'

He said soberly. 'It is sand which is highly saturated with water. It can drag a man and horse under.'

She drew her breath sharply and felt a bleak foreboding. 'Lance, how do you know your way?'

He looked at her. 'You recall that I told you three of my men know where the trunks are buried?'

'Yes.'

'This is loot from the pirating days. Brigands were on our heels. We fled New Orleans. One of my men, Jeremy Billingslea is a swamp man. He can move through here as well as a 'gator. He directed us.'

'How can you recall so much about this?'

He gazed around. 'I can't say, Elena, except that I do remember. Perhaps it comes from my years at sea.' He added, 'Also, I knew I'd return.'

'You've settled with your men about their shares?'

'Aye. When we escaped from Savannah, I got two of my ships out. I gave one ship to John Crown and the other ship to Jeremy and Maynard. I keep the buried trunks.'

'Lance, when you get these trunks, will you please place the gold in a bank?'

'I'll put it in a safer place than that.'

'Where?'

'In land,' he replied. 'I'll purchase sufficient land to plant cotton. Elena, we can double this treasure if we want.'

'You can't return to Georgia.'

He glanced at her and smiled. 'No. I have no intention of ever setting foot in Georgia again. But Natchez, Elena. There we can settle. The land looks rich and fertile.'

'Natchez,' she murmured and thought of the hours of misery she had spent there. 'It was dreadful . . .'

'I have no intention of settling in Natchez-Under-the-Hill, Elena. There's another Natchez with good people and fertile land.'

She thought of the beautiful homes she had seen above the bluff. Elena considered her future with Lance. She glanced at him. He seemed to be continually holding himself in check as if keeping a close rein on his emotions. In Savannah he had never been as quiet and tense as he was now. She thought of Dorset and Perkins waiting in Natchez.

'Another thing, Lance,' she stated. 'Dorset and Perkins have remained steadfast through this ordeal. This is your treasure, but . . .'

He tugged his reins so that the gap between them closed. He placed his hand on her shoulder. 'Elena, this gold is ours. I'd already planned to take care of Dorset and Perkins. I'll build them each houses and see that they have all they need. Perhaps I can start Perkins in a business. Have no fears on that matter. We'll take care of them to your full satisfaction.'

'Thank goodness,' she breathed while he moved away. She glanced at him and wondered if she would ever understand him. So demanding one minute, the next he could change to utmost generosity or consideration. She was certain her two servants would never again have a financial worry. She thought of how Lance had cared for Madeline Adams at the risk of his own life. He turned around to look at her.

'Those green eyes look thoughtful, Elena. What are you contemplating?'

She blushed and looked away. 'I have no intention of revealing it to you. It would only puff up your vanity.'

She expected one of his mocking replies. When none was forthcoming, she glanced at him and caught him studying her intently.

Finally they reached a stand of cypress trees. Unhesitatingly, Lance led his horse between them. Birds scattered. In the distance a keen, high cry sounded. To Elena it sounded like a shriek of doom. Her hands tightened and she rode stiffly. Ripples undulated away from the horses' hoofs and set tiny green leaves of water hyacinths wavering.

Upon entering the swamp, it appeared empty and ghostly to Elena, as if Lance and she were the only beings in an endless world of cypress, moss and water. Within seconds she realised they were surrounded with life. Birds called and moved among trees; animals howled and thrashed through water.

Each choppy splash made by the horses sounded loud. Tall cypress grew straight up with no lower branches. Moss-draped tree limbs resembled grey wraiths. Disturbed, the water smelled stagnant and fishy. A melancholy, gurgling call pierced the gloom.

'What was that?' Elena whispered.

'An egret,' Lance replied.

Nearing a fallen cypress, Elena gazed at a rotting decaying log which lay half submerged. Two dark, malevolent eyes gazed unwinkingly at her. She saw the alligator and it took all her will to keep from screaming.

The 'gator slipped into the water. This time Lance raised his pistol and fired. 'Get another pistol ready, Elena!'

He drew his second pistol and fired again.

Shots were deafening in the shrouded slough. Noisily,

birds flew from tree-tops. The 'gator began to thrash in the water as a third shot rang out. Leaving a dark stain, the reptile sank out of sight.

'Lance, when do we get out of this?' Elena whispered. She loathed to speak in normal tones fearful she might stir up other terrors.

'Not for some time, Elena.'

A terrifying prospect struck her. 'Lance, will we reach the Trace again before nightfall?'

'No.' His horse moved ahead of hers as he answered.

Contemplation of spending a night deep in a slough filled with alligators, snakes and other unpleasant creatures shook Elena. 'Lance, we cannot remain in this dreadful place!'

'Indeed, we can. We'll not head back through here in darkness.'

That quieted her because she wanted no part of travelling through the swamp at night. She gazed at the tea-coloured flat surface and shivered at prospect of what might lie below. She noticed bright green ahead and realised the water was covered with algae.

'I detest this, Lance!'

He twisted in the saddle and smiled at her. 'Do you want to . . .' His question hung in the air as his gaze went past her.

She whispered, 'What is it?'

He shook his head. 'I don't know. I thought I saw . . .' His voice trailed away and he frowned. 'It looked as if there was a horse, but I don't see anything now.'

'Parnell Tanner?' she asked.

'Aye,' Lance continued to remain twisted in the saddle to look behind them. He reached over and tugged Elena's reins. All three horses halted and Lance looked intently behind them.

Something splashed, a bird's low whistle sounded, then all was silent.

Elena wondered how anyone could follow them

through such a quagmire. It was difficult to be concerned about Tanner. Fears of the swamp and its residents crowded out all else.

Lance shifted to look at her. 'If you are afraid, Elena, would you like to ride with me? I can lead your horse.'

She shook her head grimly. 'No. I'll stay here.'

He looked at her a moment and reached over. 'Come here. I'll like this better anyway.'

Lifting her easily before him, he gathered reins to both riderless horses and they moved forward.

After a moment Lance remarked, 'Elena, this is fascinating country. There's a beauty to it I've never encountered elsewhere.'

'Beauty!'

'Yes.' He looked around. 'It's so quiet. Look at the shafts of sunlight; they're like beams of lanterns. Spanish moss softens all harshness. If the horses weren't stirring ripples, the water would be like a mirror in a flawless reflection of trees and moss. This slough is teeming with life, 'gators, snakes, turtles, lizards, possums, otters, and musk-rats. There are all kinds of birds, beautiful herons, egrets, woodpeckers, blackbirds, kites and teals. It's a marvellous place to hunt and fish.'

'I find it difficult to share your enthusiasm, Lance,' she murmured.

'Raise up slightly and glance over my shoulder.'

She did as he instructed. There was nothing behind them except swamp, trees and wildlife. A small brown bird settled on a root. Between trees a shadow moved; Elena gazed intently in its direction, but she could discern nothing unusual.

'I don't perceive anyone trailing behind us, Lance, but it's difficult to be certain. Shadows seem to move.'

'I think he's back there,' he whispered. 'I just hope there are not too many of them.'

She looked up at Lance and saw his jaw harden.

She asked, 'If he is there, what will we do?' Gazing into his glacial blue eyes, she did not see how any man could hinder Lance in his purpose.

He whispered, 'I'll not be able to answer that until the time comes, Elena. If I order you to move quickly, do so. The moment we uncover the gold, we shall be in danger.'

She twisted and peered intently over his shoulder. Suddenly he bit her ear lightly.

She yelped. 'Lance!' He grinned at her and she asked, 'What on earth . . .'

'I do not care for that long face,' he said. 'We can worry and fret later. Now, we're safe because if he shoots us, he knows he'll never find my gold.'

'Lance, how can you speak about it that way! Why didn't you put it in a bank?'

'I told you, Elena, someone was after me.'

She wondered if her life would ever be the same again. It was impossible to decide what kind of man Lance was—outlaw, renegade, tough, yet tender. He could inflame her beyond all reason. She shifted and glanced at him, noticing his thin nose beneath a wide forehead and dark brows. He looked down.

'What are you thinking, Elena?'

I was wondering what kind of man I wed.'

He smiled. 'What did you decide?'

'I can't fathom you in the least.'

He laughed and the sound lifted her spirits. Crinkles showed at the corners of his eyes. 'I'm a very simple person with some very basic desires. I think I've wanted you since you ran up to me and asked me to shoot the brigands who took your horses.'

There was a flash of overpowering hunger in his eyes; she looked down. 'You can't mean such!'

'I told you then I mean what I say. You needed to be rescued from Alfred Crowe and you needed a good sound beating . . .'

'Lance Merrick!' She straightened indignantly. It was impossible to tell when he was teasing and when he was serious.

He continued blithely, '. . . and all I can do is kiss you and adore you.' He kissed her temple lightly.

'Lance, you don't mean *those* words! You make it sound as if I can do with you whatever I wish—and that has never been so!'

She spoke with such sincerity that he threw back his head and laughed. His blue eyes filled with amusement. 'Heaven help me if I do reach that state! It's bad enough now.'

She regarded him. His teeth were white against his swarthy skin. He was handsome, more handsome than anyone she could think of. Suddenly she wished he would kiss her.

'You're teasing.' She pouted and raised her face while her heart pounded with longing for him, for his arms to tighten, to feel his mouth upon hers.

He gazed at her and laughter faded from his face. His voice was husky. 'This is one reason I've always wanted you.'

Startled, she gazed at him. 'Why?'

'Because you like to be kissed!'

'Lance Mer . . .' She started to protest, then it ended as he captured her mouth with his.

Elena clung to him while she returned his kiss with relish and abandon.

He paused and regarded her. Harshly, he spoke in cynical tones. 'This marriage should be a rewarding proposition for both of us.'

She opened her eyes and was shaken by the anger in his features. 'What, Lance?' After his dizzying kiss, it was difficult to fathom his sharp words.

He drawled laconically, 'I get the woman I have always wanted—and you get my gold.'

Aggravation replaced desire. She straightened to turn

her back to him. 'Do you want me to whisper words of love to you?'

Grasping her chin roughly, he turned her to face him. Inwardly, she quailed before his anger. 'Don't whisper that you love me unless you mean it with all your heart. I'll know, and I swear, I'll beat you if you do!'

She twisted away. 'I haven't heard any words of love from you either!' She raised her chin. 'I'll ride one of the other horses.'

He laughed and lifted her to the back of one. He gazed into her eyes and one dark eyebrow arched. 'Of all the women in the world for me to want!'

She tossed her head. 'I don't care to hear any more on the subject.'

Suddenly he tugged his reins. The horse pranced close to hers. Lance leaned over and swept her up against him to kiss her in a demanding, fiery manner that dissolved all her anger and protests.

Abruptly, he released her and looked at her. In a mocking drawl he said, 'At least you'll be a satisfactory wife on that score.' He added bitterly, 'I will always know how to stop your tirades.'

Before she could reply, he wheeled his horse away and urged it ahead swiftly. The animal stirred the water, splashing and sending waves which washed sticks and debris away from tree roots. A bird flapped skyward.

She glared angrily at his back. For over an hour Elena rode in stubborn silence, but hunger and qualms were increasing steadily.

Finally she could bear it no longer and asked, 'Lance, it's growing dark in here; when will we halt?'

'Shortly.'

Fury shook her. She decided she had received the cryptic answer out of anger and she resolved not to ask another question, but it was difficult as darkness began to descend.

A sudden roar startled her so badly she was almost

unseated. Terrified, she clung to the mane and gasped, 'What is that, Lance?'

'A 'gator,' he replied. 'He is hungry, no doubt.'

Violent trembling shook her. Somewhere behind them was a splash and she jumped again. Suddenly Lance was beside her. He lifted her in front of him while he growled, 'Come here, Elena. I know you're frightened.'

Wordlessly she slipped her arms around his narrow waist. How secure from all the terrors she felt while she clung to him.

'There, look ahead.'

Trees thinned. Grass and reeds sprang up and ahead lay a stretch of sand dotted with oaks and cypress.

They rode out of the dark slough and on to the sandbank. To their right was swamp, to the left a tangle of trees, vines and undergrowth. Stretching ahead for a reassuring distance was sand.

'I have never seen anything more welcome,' Elena breathed, then thought of the moment when Lance had appeared on the Trace. He had been an even more welcome sight, but perversely, she was not about to tell him. She waved her hand. 'Let me change horses, Lance.'

'Not necessary. We'll not ride farther tonight.' He jumped to the sand, then lifted her down. 'I'll get us a meal while you unpack the supplies we brought.' He patted a knife worn in a sheath on his hip. 'I am sufficiently hungry to eat one of those 'gators or snakes.'

When she demurred, Lance laughed. 'I will get something besides snake or 'gator to eat. It was a jest.'

She was so thankful to be on solid ground, she barely cared about the provisions. Looking over her shoulder at the gloomy, sinister swamp, a tremor shook her.

The prospect of spending the night in such a place was dreadful, but when she thought of the gold, she was willing to remain. She realised they should be near the place where it was buried; she produced the map from her saddlebag and looked at it. After a moment she looked up to discover Lance watching her with amusement.

He spoke softly. 'Do you know where the trunks are located?'

She compared the terrain with the markings on the map. She looked at him and whispered, 'I'm almost standing over them!'

'Yes, and it's good you whispered.' He strolled to her to take the map from her hands. 'This will go into the fire. I should have burned it the first night, but I forgot it.' He withdrew his pistol to hunt for food.

'Please be careful,' Elena murmured.

His aggravating grin caused her to regret her words. 'Ah,' he stated, 'if only that feeling was for my safety instead of spoken in fear I might not return to get you home through that swamp.'

'Fustian!'

He laughed and walked past her out of sight. Elena spread a blanket, gathered twigs for a fire, unpacked bread and ale. Finally she heard a shot, then shortly Lance returned. She glimpsed an ugly animal slung over his shoulder and turned away quickly while he dressed it.

'Merely a wild pig, Elena, and will be a meal fit for a king.'

'I'm so hungry, Lance.'

'This will take time, Elena. Eat some bread while we wait.'

She heaped more wood on the pile and started a blaze. Soon they had a roaring fire. Waiting for it to die slightly, Lance whittled sticks to form a spit. As soon as the meat was roasting, he continued whittling. Next he lashed sticks together to make a platform.

'What are you doing?'

'Do you care to sleep on this sand?' he asked. 'What if a 'gator comes along . . .'

'Never mind!' she interjected sharply.

His chuckle aggravated her further, but she remained silent and watched him work. He built a platform, laced the framework with large sticks and lashed them together with lengths cut from green vines. Finally he spread a blanket over it.

'There. It won't be too comfortable, but it'll be safer.'

It seemed an eternity to Elena until they finally ate the succulent pig. Afterwards, warmth from the fire, the ale, a full, delicious meal of roast pig and relaxation from worries caused by the day's trek, filled her with langour.

Lance rose and picked her up to carry her to the platform. 'Don't toss and turn too violently.'

'Where will you sleep?' she asked and felt her heartbeat increase while she waited for his answer. He gazed down at her. Flames lighted his face, throwing his hollow cheeks into shadow and casting an orange tint to his swarthy skin.

'I may join you later,' he stated and turned. She gazed after his tall figure. He wore pistol and knife, sheathed on his hips—something she had not seen him do before. He squatted before the fire and poked a log to send a spray of twinkling sparks into the air. She glanced around at the swamp so close at hand, the black water contrasting starkly with pale sand. In the distance an owl hooted.

She shifted her gaze to Lance and felt a stirring of desire. She was tempted to call to him, but the thought of Parnell Tanner's prying eyes in the darkness behind them held her back.

She relaxed and gazed at bright stars overhead. A thin sliver of moon was partially hidden by a wisp of clouds. Moss from oak and cypress limbs moved gently. She spoke and her voice was soft. 'It's beautiful here.'

He looked over his shoulder at her. 'Aye. Remote from civilization, but it's filled with life—all kinds of plants and animals, fish and fowl.'

Her thoughts changed to Tanner again. Tomorrow would bring danger. She shivered and closed her eyes.

She awakened in the night to utter darkness and Lance's hand on her shoulder.

'Elena, don't make a sound. I'm going to commence digging for the trunks. Now the real danger comes.'

Blinking, she looked up at him a moment before she comprehended the import of his words. He continued, 'I want you to ride south. We came through that swamp from the west, but we'll ride south, and later double back.'

'Lance, there is dry ground to the north. Why not go that way?

'Too dangerous, Elena. There is quicksand.'

Glancing over her shoulder, she frowned at him. 'You hunted there tonight.'

'Yes, but I didn't go far. I went due north. If I had angled back towards the Trace, I would have reached it. Listen to me, Elena. Take this pistol and go as quietly as possible. Head south until you think a quarter of an hour has passed. If I don't catch up . . .'

She stiffened and gripped his arm. 'I'll not leave without you!'

He spoke quickly. 'Yes, you will. I'll not risk Tanner catching you. There's no time for words, Elena.'

'I refuse to leave.'

He gazed at her intently. 'Elena, for God's sake . . .'

'We've come this far together—we'll see it through.'

'I know you fear the swamp, Elena, but it will be paradise compared to travel with Parnell Tanner. Go while you can.'

'No,' she stated resolutely and scrambled off the platform.

He gazed at her a moment, then motioned. 'Very well, come on.' I pray that Tanner is asleep in the mistaken notion that we'll travel farther tomorrow. Be ready to ride at an instant's notice.'

He picked up a shovel and looked down at her. 'I will dig up one trunk. We will load the saddlebags, take all we can carry and cover the trunk. The instant we finish, we'll ride into the swamp and head south.' He bent and began to shovel away sand.

Elena watched Lance as he worked. She had not wanted to leave him. She knew she could not go and be uncertain of what was happening to him.

His shovel made a metallic scraping noise. She heard his sharp intake of breath. He worked quickly and cleared the dark top of a trunk.

When he opened the lid, a pale gleam showed. She reached down and felt coins slide between her fingers.

He whispered, 'This is the trunk of gold doubloons—Spanish coins from pirating. There are ingots in other trunks and one with gems.'

She picked up a coin and gazed at an irregular shaped wafer of gold with swirls and lines in an ornate design and a large cross in the centre.

'Quickly, Elena,' he commanded. 'Pack as much as you can, but be quiet about it.'

She rose to do as he instructed. The horses were ready, tethered to the platform where she had slept.

They had made two trips from the trunk to the horses when suddenly there was a commotion behind them.

'Get on the horse and ride, Elena!' Lance demanded. He dashed to fling a saddlebag with gold across the back of one of the animals.'

'No!' she replied. She withdrew a pistol and aimed at the approaching riders.

'Elena!' he thundered while he drew his pistol and fired.

Two men rode towards them, but with the discharge of weapons, they turned back and disappeared into the dark shelter of trees in the slough.

'Get on that horse and get out of here!' Lance ordered.

'No, I would rather die here with you than ride through that swamp alone.'

The air was blue with his oaths. He crossed to her and lifted her into his arms. Elena fought against him. 'No! Lance! I'll turn around and come right back.'

'Put her down, Lance.'

From the shadows behind them came a deep voice. Lance dropped her and turned quickly to draw and fire.

Two shots blasted the night and Lance crumpled to the ground beside Elena.

CHAPTER
ELEVEN

SHE screamed and rose to her knees to grasp Lance. She turned him over and gazed in horror at the red stain spreading on his chest and shoulder. She shrieked at the man approaching her. 'You've killed him!'

Agony tore through her. Never in her life had she felt as she did that moment. She looked down at Lance and threw her arms around his inert form to sob against his chest. She heard a strong, quick heartbeat and raised to look at him again.

Men rode out of the swamp towards them and Elena looked over her shoulder again. The man had come closer and one look at his size and plaited hair and she knew it was Parnell Tanner.

Quickly she yanked off her coat and placed it against Lance's wound to staunch the flow of blood.

For the first time in her life, she realised she was truly in love. When she had thought Lance's life had ended, she felt as if her own had also. 'I do love you,' she whispered.

Momentarily, she lost all cognizance of men, gold, danger, swamp—everything, except the amazing realisation that she did love this man who was her husband!

Why had she been so foolish? She should have realised it sooner, yet when she thought of his taunting jibes and aggravating actions, she knew those had caused her to be wary of her feelings for him. Perhaps he had acted that way in his own defence. She gazed at him and thought, *I love you!*

A hand closed around her wrist and yanked her to her feet. She faced Captain Parnell Tanner. He was as large and frightening as he had appeared in Savannah. Beneath the brim of a battered hat, dark plaits stuck out from his head in all directions. His heavy black moustache and beard gave him a wild appearance.

'Mrs Merrick!' The words were filled with triumph and contempt. 'We meet again.'

Elena struggled to control her fear and raised her chin while she glared at him.

With a quick twist he pulled her close. Elena struggled futilely while he gazed down at her. 'It's a good thing I saw you in a dress in Savannah. Else I might shoot you along with Merrick and feed both of you to 'gators.'

Elena pushed against his chest. Ignoring her efforts, he asked, 'How many trunks are there?'

'I don't know.'

He placed a dirty, booted foot on Lance's chest. 'Tell me or I walk on him.'

'Get your foot off him! He is injured. There are two.'

'Two counting the one already unearthed?'

Miserably, she nodded. 'Yes,' she whispered.

He caught her chin to tilt her face upwards for a bruising, revolting kiss. He laughed at her. 'I shall take Lance Merrick's treasure and his wife!'

One of the men digging struck the lid of a trunk and called to Tanner. He turned, but kept his arm around her waist. Elena felt something brush her boot and looked down.

Lance's eyes were mere slits. He made a motion with his hand and she followed his gesture to watch him push a pistol beneath the sand. Keeping her eyes on Tanner, she moved her toe to cover the pistol. While Tanner barked commands to his men, she glanced around and saw another pistol within reach. In the same manner she pushed it beneath the sand until Tanner shifted to look at Lance.

He stated, 'I will finish Lance Merrick at last.'

'Allow me to bind his wound.'

''Tis pointless.' His words turned Elena to ice. He spoke with triumph. 'Lance and I are old enemies. It will give me great pleasure to finish him off.'

'You cannot!' she exclaimed.

She drew a sharp breath. He spoke ominously. 'After he comes around, I will put a ball through his heart. First I want to tell him that I will take you with me. You and I can enjoy his gold in Natchez-Under-the-Hill.'

Elena looked at him in anguish. Her mind raced and she spoke. 'I lied to you. I know where there is more gold. Let him live and I'll take you to it.'

'More gold?' His voice was gruff. 'You foolish baggage! Tell me where it is or I shall cause him a great deal of pain.'

'I'll have to lead you to it. Last night when we halted he instructed me. He marked a trail.' She prayed they had watched Lance go into the trees to hunt for dinner and would accept her words as truth.

His eyes narrowed. 'You can tell me now,' he stated harshly.

She shook her head. 'No. There is quicksand and you'll die if you get off the path. Leave him a horse and pistol so he can survive, and I'll lead you to the gold. I'll go with you to Natchez.'

He studied her. 'No pistol. He would hunt us down.'

'What can one injured man do against three?' she protested.

'Lance Merrick could stop five without a pistol. No, wench, I'm alive because I haven't underestimated my opponent.'

'He can't survive in this swamp without a pistol.' Elena was aware of the two buried in the sand, but anything she could get for Lance would help.

He looked down at Lance again. 'He'll survive, but

he'll not be gone from here for some time. How far is the gold?'

'He said it would be an hour's ride,' she answered. She was certain she could guess his thoughts. An hour to collect the gold, return, and kill Lance.

He looked at her. 'Yes. He can live.'

She closed her eyes. 'Thank you.'

He tilted her face upwards. 'It better be worth the bargain. I would as soon have the devil chase me after I take both you and his gold.'

She glanced down. 'Allow me to bind his wound, else he will bleed to death.'

Without a word he released her and moved towards his men who were standing over the open trunks. He stood where he could watch his men as well as Elena.

She knelt to rip the coat apart and bind strips around Lance's wound. At close study, she realised the injury was in his shoulder. She shifted so it would be difficult for Tanner to see her face. Tears splashed off her cheeks.

She whispered, 'He's watching. Don't move or stir— he thinks you're unconscious. Lance, I'll lead them north. When we go, get on a horse and leave. I'll get away from Tanner when we reach Natchez. He knows nothing about Perkins and Dorset and they can aid me to escape from him. Please get to Natchez to a doctor.'

A sob shook her. 'I love you Lance. I didn't realise it sooner—I have been so foolish. If only . . .'

She stopped at the sight of Parnell Tanner striding towards her.

'Please get away . . .'

She rose quickly and turned to face Tanner. 'Thank you,' she stated quickly.

He laughed. 'He does have a way with women!' He reached out to touch her cheek. 'Tears shed over him. Pity he does not know, but you are not the first to cry over him.' He trailed his fingers along her face. 'You're the first one he's lost his heart to. He's left the most comely wenches languishing after him. I have my spies and I know he risked life and limb to get back to you in Savannah. He said he wouldn't abandon the woman he loves.' He studied her face. 'Perhaps you're worth such a risk . . .'

His speech was a revelation. It took all her will-power to keep from looking down at Lance as she realised he must love her in return! She wanted to cry out, to throw her arms around him and sob with relief and joy, yet it was impossible. Now, when she realised her love and his, they would be separated—possibly forever.

Like a curtain closing a play, she shut her mind to all possibilities of what might have transpired if Parnell Tanner had not entered their lives. He caught her arm and growled, 'Come on.'

She hurried to keep up with Tanner's long stride as they crossed to the horses. His men loaded all the saddlebags and buried the trunks once again. Elena mounted quickly and looked again at Lance. He lay still as if unconscious and she prayed he was not, that he would get up and ride away as soon as they were out of sight.

The men mounted. Parnell Tanner turned his large black horse towards hers and reined beside her. His fingers bit into her shoulder cruelly until she cried out.

He gazed at her intently. 'If you're lying to me, wench, I shall make you pay for it.'

'I'm not lying. Unhand me!' she snapped. Her heart pounded and it took a supreme effort to keep from looking at Lance—or in the direction of the cypress where the remaining trunks were buried.

Tanner studied her intently. 'You lead the way,' he growled and released her.

Elena lifted the reins and moved in front of the men. Hot tears stung her eyes. '*Please go, Lance!*' she whispered. How long she could fool Tanner and his men was questionable. As soon as they rode very far, they would either reach quicksand or Tanner would realise she had lied about the trail.

They had packed shovels on the extra horses; they led the animals, leaving only one horse for Lance.

The land sloped upward and she entered a thick growth of trees and vines which scraped her skin. Within a short time the ground began dropping away and ahead she could see a slough.

Quicksand. She knew nothing about it—not how to recognise it or how to deal with it. Lance had uttered the word as if it ruled out all possibility of travel in this direction.

She moved northward and calculated. Lance had been gone only a short time before he fired a shot. He had returned in the direction from which he departed. She suspected he had gone straight north. The quicksand must lie to the east because he said they would go through it if they tried to reach the Trace by going north.

As if she saw an identifying mark, she announced, 'We turn here.'

Unhesitatingly, they followed.

The grey light of dawn streaked the sky and birds began to call. Ahead, mist rose from water. They approached a dark stretch of cypress. For an instant Elena considered attempting to bolt and flee through the misty swamp, but she knew it would be impossible. Noise of the horses was loud and set the water splashing and rippling.

Within minutes light showed through the trees and they emerged into a stretch of sand and sawgrass. Elena patted her horse's neck and looked at the animal thoughtfully. If they sank in quicksand, the horses would go first. She could not bear the thought of that. Tugging the reins, she halted and turned to look at Tanner.

'We leave the horses here and go on foot,' she stated forcefully and held her breath for fear he would question her actions. Quickly, she dismounted to move ahead.

Tethering the horses, all three men gathered shovels and followed. Sand stretched ahead of them. Along the length of it to their left was a tangle of trees and brush like they had just passed through.

Elena marched resolutely across the sand towards a dark bayou filled with willow and cypress.

Behind her Tanner asked, 'How much farther?'

'Not far now,' she replied and turned quickly. Streaks of sunlight were visible above treetops. The mist was dispelled.

Tears streaked Elena's cheeks. Lance should be gone by now—there had been time for him to ride away. She clenched her fists and marched across the sand as if she knew the way.

Within seconds she realised the ground had changed. There was a softness to the earth. Each step mired and made a hollow sucking noise as she withdrew her foot. Her heartbeat quickened. She plodded steadily ahead.

A few more seconds and it was as if she were wading in a muddy riverbed. It was difficult to walk and her feet were sinking deeper into gently shifting sand.

It seemed unreal, impossible to consider that she could not get out of the quagmire, yet the earth had lost all solidity. Sand became a formless ooze that pulled and held. A tremor of fear shook her, but she moved resolutely ahead.

Behind her Tanner swore. 'We're sinking!'

She looked over her shoulder and forced her voice to a lightness she did not feel. 'Only until we reach the water.'

One of the men behind her yelled, 'I can't get out of this!'

For an instant an unbridled panic surged through Elena. The contemplation of being sucked down into sand was petrifying. She wanted to run for solid ground, to flee the horrors of the insidious morass.

Oaths turned the air blue and she looked at Parnell Tanner's angry countenance. 'Go back!' he shouted to his men. 'We're getting out of this!'

Elena stood still and watched them struggle. She glanced down at her boots. The tops were covered with sand. The distance to solid ground appeared monumental.

She withdrew one foot, but the other sank farther. She put her foot down and stood quietly.

In a paroxysm of fear, one of the men shouted and ran. Tanner yelled at him as the man stumbled and sprawled forward. Parnell Tanner turned and looked into Elena's eyes.

She watched him draw a pistol and aim at her.

CHAPTER
TWELVE

SHE remained motionless. It would be useless to run even had it been possible. She faced him as he levelled the weapon.

Sunlight glinted on the pistol's silver fittings. A shot reverberated in the swamp. Birds flitted from nearby trees. The pistol flew from Tanner's grasp and Elena turned.

Beyond the sand on solid ground to her right was Lance astride the black horse!

He called. 'Don't move, Elena!'

Tanner drew another pistol and fired at Lance. Lance changed weapons and returned the shot. Tanner's body jerked backwards and he tumbled heavily into the sand.

One of his men fired at Lance. Instantly, Lance's horse whinnied loudly and disappeared into the trees.

Elena looked down. Sand covered her ankles. She took a deep breath. She wanted to run as the men had, to try to escape the prospect of being buried in the honeyed grains that shifted and closed over every object on their surface.

A scream of pure terror began to bubble in her throat, but she clenched her fists and clamped her jaw closed until it hurt. She glanced around and saw one of Tanner's men struggling wildly against sand that was chest high. The others were out of sight.

She closed her eyes. The man screamed and she was fearful she could not control her mounting panic.

'Elena!'

Lance sat astride his horse yards away—a lifetime away.

'I love you, Lance!' she cried as if that were the most important thing in the world.

He looped a rope in his hand. 'Stand still, Elena. I'll throw the rope. Grab it and wrap it under your arms.'

Tears streamed down her face. There was total silence. She could not bear to look in the direction of Tanner and his men. Lance swung the rope over his head and released it.

With a whistling sound, it snaked out and fell a few feet away. She wanted to leap for it, but Lance yelled, 'Elena! Don't move!'

She looked at him and remained still. He called, 'Let me try again. The more you move, the quicker you will sink.'

She watched the rope being drawn away and bit her lip. Perspiration poured off her temples. Her feet were completely covered by sand. She had sunk almost to the calves of her legs.

Hysteria threatened, but she fixed her attention on Lance and clamped her jaw shut to prevent crying out.

'Elena! Here it comes again.'

The rope sailed through the air. She reached up and her fingers locked around it.

Hope leapt within and she cried, 'I have it!'

'Drop it over your head and under your arms so the strain will be on your shoulders,' he instructed calmly.

She did as he commanded.

Lance wrapped loops of rope around the pommel of his saddle.

She called, 'Lance, I'll fall before my feet come free.'

He dismounted and stood at the horse's head to keep the rope taut. 'Now, move slowly and carefully. Twist and lie down on your back. Quicksand is filled with water and buoyant if you don't struggle against it. Lie on your back and don't panic if you sink slightly. I can pull you out and you won't go completely under.'

She looked at him intently. Strips of her black coat were wrapped around his shoulder. His dark curls were tangled and the buckskin clothing was stained with blood. He was the most wonderful sight in the world and she longed to be safe in his arms.

She took a deep breath and slowly turned to stretch on her back.

'Relax, Elena. You won't sink as much.'

The sand was soft, clinging to every inch of her wherever it touched. Cool, fluid and yielding, it oozed and shifted. She felt it rise, touch her cheeks, close around her ears. She shuddered and shut her eyes.

'That's it!' Lance encouraged. 'We'll take it slowly; hang on.'

The rope tightened and she locked her hands on it beneath her chin. She began to move. The rope bit into her arms and scraped across her chin, yet she clung tightly. The only sanity in a world of terror was his strong, calm voice.

Slowly she was dragged backwards. Elena could see only the rope and sky overhead, yet she felt the continual shift of sand as she moved. Lance called steadily to her, but it was impossible to gauge how much farther she had to go.

His voice sounded louder. He no longer shouted, but spoke in normal tones. Suddenly Lance's arms closed around her and lifted her up against him.

A sob racked her body and she shook until her teeth chattered. His arms squeezed the breath from her, but she simply clung to him and sobbed.

Finally she realised how tightly she was being held and pushed lightly against his chest. 'You will hurt your arm . . .'

'I don't give a damn, Elena,' he answered gruffly. 'Nothing could hurt as much as losing you . . .'

The words sent a thrill through her. She stood on

tiptoe and pulled his face down to kiss him. He returned the kiss with such ardour that she forgot all the past moments of horror.

Finally he released her and gazed at her. 'Elena, I was afraid I would not be able to rescue you.' His eyes darkened. 'I almost didn't.'

'How did you find us?'

'I have followed behind all the way.'

His words sent a wave of shock through her. 'Oh, Lance, if only I had known that you were near . . .'

He growled. 'I couldn't take on all three of them. Parnell would have killed you. I couldn't decide what else to do, but let you lead them into that sand. When he drew his pistol and aimed at you . . .' He pulled her close again. 'You don't know how much I love you!'

He looked down again. 'Let's get away from here.' He shifted as if to pick her up, but Elena pushed against him quickly. 'I can get on the horse without aid.'

After she had climbed into the saddle, Lance swung up behind her. He looped the rope over the pommel and slipped his arm around her waist to hold her tightly.

They returned to collect the horses. All were laden with bags of gold. Lance spoke softly. 'There is enough gold here to allow us to wed properly, take a wedding trip and establish a home before I return to get the rest.'

She shuddered. 'Lance, I can't bear the thought of you returning to this place. It seems filled with disaster. Tanner came to such a terrible end.'

'Elena, Parnell Tanner was a wicked, evil man. He would have killed you eventually. I want you to forget all of this.'

She shifted to look up at him. 'I can ride another horse.'

He shook his head. 'Not yet.' His arm tightened possessively around her waist.

'Lance, why didn't you tell me? If only I had known that you loved me . . .'

His blue eyes were solemn. 'You could have destroyed me. I've always felt that someday you'd return my love . . .'

She slipped an arm around his neck. Careful to avoid bumping his injured shoulder, she pulled him close to kiss him.

He shifted and looked at her solemnly. 'You asked me once if I feared anything.'

She nodded. 'I recall you said only one . . .' She drew a sharp breath and he nodded.

'Yes, Elena. There are many things I am cautious about, many I do not like or am willing to fight, but the only deep fear I've had was that I'd never have your love.'

Forgetting his shoulder, she threw both arms around his neck to kiss him.

Elena looked up into Lance's blue eyes and repeated the marriage vows she had once uttered to him before, so long ago in Savannah.

She thought how different this ceremony was from the other—the church with sunlight streaming through high stained glass windows, Dorset and Perkins nearby, Lance dressed in an elegant black coat and champagne-coloured breeches while she wore a white lace dress and tulle veil.

Lance raised her hand to slip a gold band on her finger. He paused and looked down at the hairpin still bent around her slender finger. When his brown fingers began to slip the pin off, Elena could not bear it. She reached out quickly and touched his wrist.

He glanced at her in surprise and Elena shook her head. She could not part with that first ring. It had bound her to him forever and she wanted it to remain on her hand.

He smiled and slipped the gold band on to her finger against the hairpin. Kissing her briefly, he took her arm and they walked down the aisle into Natchez sunshine.

After receiving good wishes from the few new friends they had made in the two weeks since they had returned from the Trace, Elena said farewell to her two faithful servants. Lance took her hand and they dashed to his waiting carriage.

Once inside, he took the reins to drive the open vehicle towards the Natchez home he had purchased. Instead of turning at the corner as he should, he continued towards the Trace. Elena looked at him questioningly.

'I have a surprise,' he stated and dropped his arm around her shoulders to draw her close. She raised her lips for a kiss, and settled in contentment against him while they left Natchez behind.

'You are not taking me over the Trace again, are you?' she asked suddenly, aware that he was capable of almost anything.

He chuckled. 'No, Elena.' He turned and looked at her solemnly. 'You could have had a wedding trip to almost any city in the world.'

She shook her head. 'It'll be a long time before I want to leave Natchez. I feel at home here, Lance, because of you. We can start our life together here.'

He kissed her. She pushed against him lightly and laughed. 'You'd better keep your eyes on the new team of horses. This carriage will be off the road!' He grinned and looked at the well-matched, glossy bays while Elena thought of the house in Natchez he had purchased. Made of cypress with a sloping roof, it had a long gallery and beautiful fan transoms with tall magnolia trees beside the verandah.

She had loved it at first sight and contemplation of dwelling there with Lance set her heart pounding. She looked at him impatiently and wondered why he was delaying taking her home.

He caught her glancing at him and laughed. 'I see fire beginning to flash in those green eyes.'

She shook her head. 'I love you too much for anything you do to aggravate me!'

'Oh ho! That I will remind you about, Mrs Merrick.' Within minutes he turned the carriage off the road on to an open meadow.

'Lance, what on earth!' Elena clutched the side of the carriage as it bounced wildly.

He grinned. 'You'll see.'

Within seconds they reached a horse, saddled and tethered beneath a sycamore. When Lance halted the carriage, he jumped down and swung Elena into his arms to carry her to the horse. He mounted behind her.

'I'll stop asking questions,' she stated, 'since I see it's to no avail.'

'Not much longer, Elena.' He raised her hand in his and kissed it. He studied her fingers. 'Why do you want that hairpin around your finger?'

She spoke softly. 'Because Lance, I became yours with it, that moment in Savannah, even though I was too giddy to realise it.'

He kissed her temple. 'Ah, Elena, how I love you!'

She felt him shake and glanced up sharply.

'Why are you laughing?'

'Because, my love, I'll always remember riding up to find you at death's door in that swamp, being fired on by a brigand and sinking into a quagmire—and the first thing you did was to yell "I love you".'

She blushed. 'Oh, Lance, I've been so foolish . . .'

His blue eyes twinkled. 'Just what I told you long ago.'

He tugged the reins, dropped to the ground and lifted her down beside him. She gasped with delight.

They were on a high bluff overlooking a bend of the Mississippi River. The land spread out below them in green, rolling hills covered with forest. Along the river-bank willows hung gracefully above the brown water.

She glanced around. Three large oaks shaded the sunny slope where they stood. The moss-draped limbs added an ethereal softness to dark branches. Elena watched Lance reach behind the saddle and get a blanket. He moved the horse away and spread the blanket on the ground.

While she observed his actions, she thought how handsome he was. Her heartbeat quickened as she gazed at his swarthy skin and glints in his black curls. She longed to feel his arms around her. She felt as if she had waited an eternity for this man. 'Lance . . .'

He faced her across the blanket, then strolled to her and lifted her into his arms. He held her close and smiled.

'Welcome home, love.'

She asked, 'What are you talking about, Lance?'

'I have purchased this land for you.' He looked beyond her at the fields below the bluff. 'This will be our home, Elena.'

She looked at him in surprise. He spoke. 'See those fields—I'll have them cleared and planted with cotton soon.'

He turned and pointed in the direction of the grassy slope behind them. 'The house will go here. We'll build whatever you would like.'

She wound her arms around his neck and murmured languorously, 'The house is lovely, Lance.'

Hunger flared in the depths of his blue eyes. Pressed against his chest, Elena felt his quickened heartbeat match her own.

'Now, Mrs Merrick, let me show you the bedroom,' he whispered huskily. Lance lowered her gently to the blanket to take her in his arms.

Elena turned eagerly and clung to this man who had brought her the utmost happiness.